The
Homecoming

EARL HAMNER, JR.

THE

HOMECOMING

A Novel
About Spencer's Mountain

RANDOM HOUSE

New York

For Scott and Carrie

It is remembered in my family that on Christmas Eve of 1933 my father was late arriving home. That, along with the love he and my mother bestowed upon their eight red-headed offspring, is fact. The rest is fiction.

The
Homecoming

ONE

ALL day the cold Virginia sky had hung low over
Spencer's Mountain. It was a leaden, silent, moist
presence. It promised snow before the fall of night.

Looking from her kitchen window, Olivia Spencer
observed the ashen sky. It did not *feel* like Christmas.
That moment which had always come in other years,
that mingled feeling of excitement and promise which
she called The Christmas Spirit, had evaded her.
Christmas had always been a time of rejuvenation to
Olivia, a time to reaffirm her faith in God's goodness,
to enjoy the closeness of friends and family; a time to
believe in miracles again.

She could trace the root of her depression. It had
begun this morning when she had gone to the upstairs
hall where she kept her Christmas Cactus in a spot
where a maximum of winter sun filtered in through
the window. But one of the children had broken a

window pane, and she found the plant dead, frozen in the harsh draft that had flowed over it all night long. Its full pink buds were wilted, stilled before they had even opened, the oval segments of each stalk crumbling and falling away at her touch.

The dead plant had somehow set the tone for all that was to follow in the day. The blustery cold had kept the children indoors, a complaining, bickering, grumbling mob, constantly underfoot and in her way as she tried to clean the house. She had no patience with holiday frivolity. She wished for spring.

This year if it were not for the children she might even be tempted to treat Christmas as just another day. Prospects being what they were, it could well turn out to be just another day, no matter how hard she tried to make it festive.

As Olivia watched from her window the snow began. It arrived in a thin curtain which appeared at the edge of the barn, then swept down across the yard and over the house. More curtains of snow followed, each one thicker, heavier with flakes, until the downfall became an opaque drift of cold blue-white crystals. Enclosed in the privacy of storm, the house seemed an island of warmth and safety.

"Y'all children want to see somethen pretty?" she called.

The children, all eight of them, converged on the

[4]

window, and crowded their red heads around their mother. They looked out toward the barn and past it across field and woodland to where Spencer's Mountain was growing dim, softly outlined through the cold, gently drifting whiteness.

On the tallest limb of the crab-apple tree perched a cardinal. His scarlet plumage flashed a single stroke of bright color in a landscape of winter grey, snow white and ice blue.

"That red bird is goen to freeze tonight," observed Luke. Luke was ten, the handsome one with hair almost the same shade as the red bird in the crab-apple tree.

"He won't freeze," said Olivia. "A red bird has got the knack of surviven winter. He knows it too. Otherwise he'd of headed South with the wrens and the goldfinches and the bluebirds back when the leaves started to turn."

She looked back to the yard again, where the clothesline posts were turning to tall and sheeted ghosts.

"I wish my daddy could fly," said Shirley solemnly. Shirley was the sensitive one with a head covered with auburn ringlets. Her father claimed that she was prettier than Shirley Temple and often vowed that if he could get her to Hollywood, California, she would be bound to become a movie star.

Her wish that her father could fly like a bird was met with howls of laughter. Shirley pouted prettily and looked at her brothers and sisters with an injured air.

"If he could fly then he wouldn't have to wait for the bus," explained Shirley.

"Daddy go flyen around, somebody liable to think he's a turkey buzzard and shoot him down," said Mark.

"Y'all leave Shirley alone," warned Olivia when the children began laughing and making faces at her. Olivia hugged the little girl to her and said, "Don't you worry about your daddy. He's goen to be home for Christmas. You stop fretten about it."

"He won't be here if he stops off at Miss Emma's and Miss Etta's," said Becky, who was thirteen and had a mind of her own.

"Huh!" said Olivia, with the contempt she reserved for alcohol, those who sold it and those who had a weakness for it. "The day your daddy spends Christmas Eve with two old lady bootleggers is the day I walk out of this house."

"Where'll we go, Mama?" asked Pattie-Cake, and began to cry. Pattie-Cake was eight and took everybody literally.

"Your daddy's goen to be home," Olivia assured Pattie-Cake. "Y'all just stop worryen."

The Homecoming

Clay Spencer could only be with his family on weekends. When something called "the Depression" had happened in Washington or New York or some distant place, the soapstone plant had closed down, and all the men in the village had to find other jobs and other ways of making a living for their families. Clay had found work as a machinist at the Du Pont Company in Waynesboro, which was forty miles away. He had no car, so every Friday night he would take the Trailways bus to Charlottesville, transfer to the southbound bus that let him off at Hickory Creek on Route 29, which was also called The Seminole Trail. From there Clay would walk the remaining six miles or hitchhike if a car happened to go past.

He wouldn't stop at the Staples place tonight, Olivia thought. Not on Christmas Eve. She sometimes thought she would enjoy setting sticks of dynamite under Miss Emma and Miss Etta Staples' house and blowing it sky high. She enjoyed the vision of the stately, decayed old house and its shelves of Mason jars filled with the notorious "Recipe" the old ladies distilled, being blown right off the map.

Olivia realized that the children were still gazing at her with concern.

"Come on," she said, "there's work to do. Who's goen to crack walnuts for my applesauce cake?"

Everybody wanted to crack walnuts. Olivia realized

[7]

their willingness stemmed from the fact that it would be an excuse to get out into the snow.

"Run along then," she said.

The children scattered, collecting jackets and sweaters and overshoes and caps and scarves and hammers.

"You look after everybody, Clay-Boy," called Olivia as the children filed out onto the back porch. "You're the oldest."

"Yes ma'am," answered Clay-Boy, a thin boy of fifteen with a serious, freckled face topped by an unruly shock of darkening corn-colored hair.

If Clay-Boy had any wish in life it was that his mother would stop reminding him that he was the oldest. It took all the fun out of things to be constantly reminded that he was a combination policeman, referee, guardian and nursemaid to his younger brothers and sisters.

"I'm like some old mother duck," thought Clay-Boy as he made his way through the new snow to the barn, followed by Matt, Becky, Shirley, Mark, Luke, John and Pattie-Cake.

Each of the children had red hair, but on each head the shade was a little different. Clay-Boy's hair was the color of dry corn shucks. Matt's was the red of the clay hills. Becky's straight bob was the pink of a sunset. Shirley's curls were auburn. Luke's hair was the russet of autumn leaves. Mark's was reddish blond. John's ringlets were a golden red and Pattie-Cake's little ponytail was orange.

The children were slender of bone and lean. Some of them were freckled and some were not. Some had the brown eyes of their father, and some had their mother's green eyes, but on each of them there was a stamp of grace in build and movement. It was this their father voiced when he said, as he often did, "Every one of my babies is a thoroughbred."

Reaching the barn, Clay-Boy lifted the latch and opened the door to the storeroom. The children flowed in past him like heedless, impatient baby chicks.

"Y'all watch yourselves," hollered Clay-Boy. "Somebody gets hurt I'll get the blame!"

But they paid him no mind. They were hopeless.

"Lordy God," he grumbled. "I'll be glad when y'all grow up and learn sense."

The barn was cold, and smelled of hickory smoke and fresh hay and drying wood and mice. Clay-Boy pulled the burlap sack filled with black walnuts from the bin where he had stored them in October, slung the sack over his shoulder and started back toward the house.

"Y'all can bring some stove wood if you don't want to freeze tonight," he called over his shoulder to the pack of children behind him.

Each child followed him to the house carrying a few

sticks of wood. They piled it in the woodbox on the back porch, then each of them took a handful of walnuts as Clay-Boy passed them out.

As they worked, Pattie-Cake announced proudly, "I wrote a letter to Santa Claus."

John, who was nine and practical, said, "It won't do you a speck of good."

"How come?" asked Pattie-Cake, her lower lip already beginning to quiver.

"How you goen to get it to him? He's clean at the North Pole. No letter goen to get to the North Pole by tonight."

"What'll I do, Clay-Boy?" asked Pattie-Cake anxiously.

"You give it to me, honey," said Clay-Boy. "I'll take it down to the post office and send it Special Delivery."

"I'm much obliged to you, Clay-Boy," said Pattie-Cake gratefully.

Becky snickered and whispered to Shirley, "He's just pacifyen her."

"Shut up, Becky," warned Clay-Boy, "before I spank your bottom till it's red, white and blue."

"You just try it, big boy," replied Becky. She made a threatening fist, and stuck out her tongue.

"What did you ask Santa Claus to bring you, honey?" asked Matt, who was the industrious one and had already cracked six walnuts.

"One whole page in the *Sears, Roebuck Catalogue*," replied Pattie-Cake. "A whole page of dolls."

"I been thinken about writen to him myself," said John.

"What you asken for, John?"

"A piano and a pair of ice skates," answered John.

"That man can't carry no piano down the chimney," said Mark. "He ain't hardly any bigger than Mama, little old fat fellow with a big belly. I seen his picture."

"Huh!" said Becky in a superior way.

"What's that 'huh' for?" asked Clay-Boy.

"Everybody's so ignorant around here," said Becky. She looked at her brothers and sisters with a lofty air of disgust.

"What makes you say that?" asked Matt.

"Believen in Santa Claus," snorted Becky. "There's no such thing. It's just somethen Mama and Daddy made up."

"I don't believe you," said Pattie-Cake and blinked her eyes at Becky indignantly.

"That's because you're ignorant," cried Becky.

Pattie-Cake began to weep. Large salty tears flowed down her cheeks and fell on the one walnut she still struggled to crack.

"You're bad, Becky," said Matt, and gave her a push that sent her sprawling off the porch. Becky rose from the ground, clenched her fists and walked grimly back to Matt.

"Son, you're goen to be sorry you did that," she threatened. She spit into her palms, rubbed her hands together and then made fists again.

"You want to make somethen out of it?" asked Matt, with a teasing grin.

"You're double-durned right I'm goen to make something out of it," said Becky, standing her ground, fists poised like a picture she had seen once of John L. Sullivan.

"I'm goen to tell Mama you said a bad word," announced Shirley. "And she'll wash your mouth out with Octagon soap."

"You little old mealy-mouth thing," said Becky contemptuously. "I hope you get a bad cold and sneeze your eyes loose."

"You watch it, young lady," warned Clay-Boy. "You just watch that biggity talk!"

"I'm not goen to have anything to do with any of you," said Becky. She stuck her nose up in the air and walked off into the yard, catching snow flakes on the tip of her tongue.

Why did they always give her nothing but trouble, she wondered. Why was it so difficult to be a thirteen-year-old girl? She decided that next summer when she was working in the garden she would chop off one of her toes with a hoe. It would seem an accident. Maybe then they would feel sorry for her and stop picking on her all the time. Maybe then they might even like her.

On the porch the other children had nearly filled the cup with walnuts.

"There is too a Santa Claus, isn't there, Clay-Boy?" asked Pattie-Cake.

"Sho'," answered Clay-Boy reassuringly. "Wait'll in the mornen. You'll see."

Clay-Boy wished he had not spoken so affirmatively. He knew that his mother had not had the money to buy any presents for the children. Their only chance for presents from Santa Claus was if their father brought them, and Clay-Boy had learned enough to know the many temptations that lay in the path of a man who had labored hard all week and who had just received his pay.

Olivia had already started her applesauce cake when the children trooped in with the walnuts. The kitchen steamed with the aroma of cloves, cinnamon and nutmeg. At the old wood-burning cooking range Olivia was stirring the applesauce and singing "O Little Town of Bethlehem."

"Mama's got The Christmas Spirit!" exclaimed John.

"Just come up on me all of a sudden," declared Olivia. "Clay-Boy, you go get the tree!"

"Yes ma'am," answered Clay-Boy.

"I'm goen too," announced Becky.

"No, you are not," replied Olivia. "You're stayen here and helpen me."

"I want to go!" insisted Becky.

"A girl's place is to help in the kitchen. Cutten down trees is men's work."

"Let Shirley help. She's such a prissy butt!"

"I am not a prissy butt," rejoined Shirley indignantly.

"I'm tryen to get Christmas ready and you children aren't helpen me," scolded Olivia. "Now get busy on those dishes. Becky, you wash. Shirley, you dry."

Hands in the belt loops of her blue jeans, Becky sauntered to the sink in imitation of Gene Autry, the Singing Cowboy. When the water from the faucet was running full and splashing into the sink, she thought the noise was loud enough to cover her voice and she swore vehemently, "Damnit!"

A swat on the seat of her blue jeans told her that the water had not been loud enough, and as Olivia glowered at her, Becky wondered how many dishes she might break and make it seem accidental.

She wept silently into the dish water and wished for her daddy. If he were here he would hold her in his arms, tell her she was a Crackerjack, and give her whiskey-flavored kisses. She resolved that when she

[14]

grew up she would get a job at Waynesboro too and ride the Trailways bus and come home every Friday night and blow whiskey breath right in her mother's face. If Mama said a word she'd just tell her to like it or lump it.

TWO

AHEAD of him Spencer's Mountain loomed snow-white, pine-green, arched with the misty blue of a cold, snowy December afternoon. The mountain housed all those things mysterious to Clay-Boy. There were caves there where, long ago, boys had been lost and never found. One of the caves contained a hidden lake, so deep that if a stone were dropped from the rim a person could count to five before the sound of the splash would travel back. The mountain was home to monstrous rattlesnakes, owls, bobcats, bear, all manner of rodents, but its special fascination for Clay-Boy lay in the fact that it was the range of a legendary white deer imbedded in his memory from the earliest tales he had heard from his Grandfather Spencer.

"Up on the mountain, when I was a boy, there used to be a big old buck deer that was white all over and had pink eyes. Lots of folks that never laid eyes on

*him used to claim there wasn't no such thing. Some of
them even claimed he was a ghost. I don't say one way
or another, ghost or flesh. All I know is I have laid
eyes on him.*"

The story would be told at family gatherings when
the men would congregate in the living room to drink
whiskey and swap yarns.

"*Oh, Papa, that deer is dead and gone. I never heard
of one liven longer than ten or eleven years.*"

"*He's up there. You mark my words!*"

Clay-Boy had never seen the albino deer, but his
grandfather's stories were seared in his memory. Now
as he entered the old wood road which wound its way
to the top of the mountain, he was conscious that he
was in the deer's territory and almost automatically
began keeping an eye out for tracks or droppings that
might alert him to the deer's presence. If indeed the
deer existed at all.

The wilderness silence and the snow silence de-
scended upon the boy as he trudged upward through
a landscape of leafless trees, their dark sleeping limbs
starkly etched against the virgin snow. As the woods
filled up with snow, each dazzling crystal stuck where-
ever it fell and the road turned into a fantastic aisle
of white carpet through crystal columns and ermine
arches. The crystals were small, the kind his grandfather always predicted foretold a deep and powdery

snow, and his grandfather spoke with authority, for he knew how to read the messages hidden in moon and cloud and wind.

The boy was warm in his father's old sheepskin jacket. The jacket smelled of his father, a faint scent of tobacco smoke, the remembrance of gunpowder, for Clay always wore the jacket when he went hunting for quail or rabbit or wild turkey which the family had come to depend upon increasingly for food since the Depression had arrived.

Clay-Boy pushed his hands into the pockets of the jacket and found in one of them the remains of a pack of Camels and a box of matches. He had experimented with smoking before and found it to his liking. Removing a crumpled cigarette from the pack, he lit it and drew the smoke into his lungs. When he exhaled, the blue smoke drifted off through the sharp wintery air and dissolved in the snow. Clay-Boy couldn't decide what it was he liked about smoking. He wondered how he looked holding the cigarette between his thumb and forefinger, the way his father did. He fancied he probably looked like a man.

Clay-Boy thought of his father ruefully. Clay Spencer was a hard man to measure up to. Like all the Spencer men he was a crack shot, a good provider for his family, an honest "look-em-in-the-eye" man, an enthusiastic drinker, a prodigious dancer, a fixer of things, a builder, a singer of note, a teller of bawdy stories, a kissing, hugging, loving man whose laughter would shake the house, and who was not ashamed to cry. He seemed to his son an outsized man, bigger than life. It was with a sense of wonder that the boy observed his own body's growth and found his head reaching, it seemed to him almost overnight, to a level with his father's head, shoulder to shoulder, eye to eye.

As much as he wanted to be like his father, something pulled Clay-Boy in another direction. He knew his father sometimes thought him strange. Clay would walk into the boys' room and observe his son intently writing with a pencil in his school tablet. The other children would be in the yard playing Giant Step, or Capture the Flag, or baseball. Clay would look at the boy, vaguely troubled.

"What you up to, son?"

"Homework," Clay would lie, and cover the tablet. How could he possibly tell his father that he was writing a story? Writers had names like Alfred Lord Tennyson, Percy Bysshe Shelley, and William Makepeace Thackeray. How could his father possibly understand that he, Clay-Boy Spencer, felt some strange compulsion to write his thoughts into a tablet meant for school work? He had told no one, and hid the things he wrote away from the world like some secret vice.

He was overcome for a moment with a sense of

futility. There was so much he wanted to tell, so much he felt that he could only tell in the words he wrote on the tablet. But he was reaching now toward manhood. The time would soon be near when he must put away childish things and learn to be a man, to make a living and provide for a family.

He watched the wood softly receive the white snow blanket, gently transforming rock and bush and clay bank into new and magical formations. He crossed a small ice-crusted stream where beneath the opaque, frost-fingered ice the water gurgled slowly. Skirting the stream, he continued the upward climb.

Halfway up the mountain Clay-Boy paused to rest. He looked up, gauging how much farther he had to climb. From where he stood, he could see, dimly outlined through the snow, the promontory which was the site of his father's house. The house was not really a house, but a dream his father had. It was Clay's dream to build a house with his own hands, a house his wife and children could see being constructed, a house that would give strength and love to their lives because they would see the strength and love with which it was built.

"I can see it now, a white house with green shutters on the windows. Your mama sitten up there on the front porch resten of a Sunday. Your mama will plant flowers down the walk on either side and I'll put in a bed of grass where my babies can play."

The Homecoming

Clay had promised the house to Olivia on their wedding night and had shown her where he would build it, on the summit of Spencer's Mountain in the same spot where his mother and father's old cabin had long since rotted away.

In olden times Spencer's Mountain had belonged to Grandfather Spencer. As each of his sons became twenty-one the old man would give him his choice of land so that by the time Clay, the youngest, reached the age of manhood, the mountain had been divided into nine plots, and Clay fell heir to the original cabin. Only Clay, of all the brothers, held on to his share of the mountain.

As the years went by, the vision of the house he would some day build never left Clay Spencer's mind. Every time he passed the site he would imagine the house. In his dreams it was always etched against a summer sky, the house a solid frame structure with many rooms, painted white, the windows trimmed with green shutters, and a wisp of smoke trailing from the chimney. The vision was so real to him that he could almost hear the children's voices inside or see Olivia's face at the window.

Yet, as strong as this vision was, he had never gotten beyond excavating the basement; this he accomplished every summer, only to have it fill in again during the fall and winter rains. Each summer he would attack the hole again with the intention that this year he would at least get the foundation laid during the week-ends when he did not have to work at the mill. When the Depression came and Clay went off to Waynes-boro to work, progress on the house stopped entirely.

Snow had covered the site of his father's dream house when Clay-Boy arrived there. He had saved himself the trouble of toting an ax, knowing his father kept one with the other tools he stored on the moun-tain to build the house with. Clay-Boy found the snow-shrouded mound where the tools were stored. With mittened hands he pushed aside the frozen tar-paulin and took out the ax. Holding the ax carefully, the way his father had taught him to carry it on slip-pery ground, Clay-Boy set out across an open field which in his grandfather's time had been planted in corn. Next he passed through what had been an or-chard. A few of the old peach and apple trees still remained, but they were old and neglected and bore little fruit. His grandfather had cleared the land to the edge of a pine forest. Reaching the edge of the stand of pine, Clay-Boy skirted the forest for nearly half a mile and continued on to another large open field which had formerly been used to pasture cattle.

The place was a high meadow. In the summer it was filled with the scent of sun-hot clover, but now it was a long and lonely expanse of snowy field. The meadow was dotted with many trees, but Clay-Boy went directly to one of them. The tree was six feet tall, a perfectly symmetrical eastern hemlock. Even in the brisk winter air, Clay-Boy could smell its pungent evergreen scent. He and Mama and the children had come upon it last summer on a berry-picking expedition. They had agreed, even that long ago, that this particular hemlock was to be this year's Christmas Tree. Whenever some chance brought them to the mountain, they had visited it and envisioned it standing in the corner of the living room, festooned with ropes of silver tinsel and hung with ornaments of red and green and gold, crowned at its very tip with the silver star which had been in Grandma Spencer's family for generations.

Getting down on his hands and knees, Clay-Boy crawled under the tree to examine the trunk. He discovered there a secret world. The upper branches of the tree had caught the snow so that none had fallen on the earth below. A thick circle of needles covered the ground and the lower limbs dropped at their tips to form a small, tent-like enclosure. No wind reached him there and Clay-Boy felt the way he imagined it might be in an igloo. There were rabbit droppings in spots and a small pile of pine wood knots. Clay-Boy guessed that his father might have thrown the pine knots there to hide them, for they caught flame readily and made good starting wood for a fire. Clay-Boy was still for a moment, imagining the feeling of sanctuary a small animal might enjoy if it sought refuge there or stopped for a moment to rest.

Clay-Boy was examining the base of the tree to determine just where to make his first cut with the ax when in the periphery of his vision he detected movement.

He felt an involuntary sense of fright because he had thought himself to be alone.

He turned and drew in his breath excitedly at what he saw. At the edge of the pine forest was a female deer. She stood, Clay-Boy guessed, about shoulder high. Her coat for the winter had turned a bluish-brown, except for the inside of her ears and the throat patch, which were pure white. She was fully grown and looked to weigh from a hundred and fifty to two hundred pounds. She raised her head, her black, moist nose pointing to the sky, and since he was downwind from her, Clay-Boy knew that she had no idea of his presence.

Satisfied that the field was free of danger, the doe started across it in rhythmic leaps. From time to time she would stop and gaze about searchingly. Clay-Boy wondered what had brought her there. Usually the deer gathered in herds and spent the winter months together for protection. Perhaps she was late in season and might still be seeking a male deer. Or it could be that she had been separated from the herd by a dog or hunters or a wildcat, and she was trying to locate the herd again before the dark winter night set in.

Spellbound by the sight of the deer, Clay-Boy lost all sense of time. The doe continued toward him, in a graceful, undulating motion, setting her thin hooves down in the snow in a sure and elegant unison. Clay-Boy was glad he had not brought a gun. The family could have used the venison, and he might have been tempted to shoot her.

He decided that she was simply out for her evening feed, for about a hundred feet from where Clay-Boy hunched in his hideaway, the doe stopped and began to graze on the tips of a persimmon grove. Some frost-blackened persimmons still clung to the tree. She ate these first, swallowing seeds and all. Then she began chewing off the softer and younger twigs and branches. Clay-Boy drew in his breath and caught the faint scent of wild, musky game.

Perhaps she heard him breathe. Perhaps the wind turned. In an instant the doe perceived Clay-Boy's presence. In a single motion she flagged her tail, lifted her head and sprang into the air. When she touched the earth again her legs carried her swiftly forward.

As swiftly as she bolted away, the deer came to a halt and seemed to sink into the snow. Watching her struggle, Clay-Boy wondered what had brought her down, and then he saw that she had become trapped in a deadfall. He and his father had thrown the collection of dead limbs and branches into the deep gully last summer when they had cut down an old water oak for firewood. They had filled the gully with the limbs, hoping to stop the erosion which was setting in, and with the snow covering the deadfall, the doe had mistaken the crust of snow for solid ground. Now she was trapped, her legs plunged through layer after layer of dead branches. She thrashed about wildly in an attempt to free herself, but she succeeded only in sinking deeper and deeper into the mesh of dead tree limbs. Trapped, earthbound, subject to gravity, some magic quality went out of the animal. Clay-Boy regretted that her flight had been halted, and he debated whether he might be of any use to her or whether she might free herself unaided.

It would have been a simple matter to dispatch her with one blow of the ax, and the thought occurred to Clay-Boy because he was the son of a hunter. But that was not the boy's intention as he rushed toward the deer, ax in hand. He had thrown many of the branches there himself, knew the direction in which they lay and figured that by dragging some of the heavier limbs out of the pile he might free the doe.

At his approach she thrashed about with renewed vigor, throwing her head from side to side, watching him with haunted eyes. Closer now, he could see the slender grace of her brown face, the dark anguished eyes circled with white fur.

"Easy, girl," he called in a soothing voice, but the doe showed her distrust by renewing her struggle and fighting the deadfall.

Much of the snow which had been encrusted on the surface of the deadfall, shaken loose by the struggling deer, had sifted down so that Clay-Boy could tell exactly which limbs held her so securely. When he was within arm's reach of the doe she seemed to be suddenly paralyzed, or else so resigned to fate that she lay completely still, her eyes blinking with hatred. Clay-Boy reached out and grasped the end of a limb. When he began tugging at it, the doe lifted her head sharply, throwing foamy saliva on his jacket.

"It's all right, lady," he said softly, making himself move slowly, hoping not to frighten the doe further.

Slowly he extricated a limb from the pile, but it was not enough to free the doe. He threw it aside, returned to the deadfall and pulled another limb free. He loosened another and another. Suddenly the doe heaved her body upward, freeing one leg for a moment, only to sink again into the mass of limbs.

Through the swirling snow Clay-Boy felt the day shift. The unseen sun was moving down toward the horizon. Night would be falling soon. He did not want to be caught on the mountain after dark. It would take him hours to remove the entire deadfall, so Clay-Boy knelt in the snow to examine the way in which the doe was caught to see what limbs might be most strategically removed.

Peering into the maze of tree limbs, his attention was drawn to a sound. It was a high, nasal, angry snort. Clay-Boy jerked his head around but at first saw nothing which could have made the sound. Then something moved across the snow-swept field, a massive, albino buck, and even at this distance Clay-Boy could see its pink eyes grown red with anger.

From the number of its points Clay-Boy knew that the buck was young, not the legendary white deer of his grandfather's tales. It was sure, however, to be a son or a grandson. Because natural-colored deer will avoid an albino, and because the buck still retained his rack of antlers, Clay-Boy judged that the buck was still in rut and might have been enticed there by the scent of the doe. If that was the case, Clay-Boy knew that the normally placid and furtive animal could be dangerous.

One moment the albino buck was standing quite still, a second later he stamped the ground twice, and then charged.

Clay-Boy felt his mouth go dry. A rush of adrenaline sent his heart pounding and his feet flying. The nearest cover was the Christmas Tree he had intended to cut. Throwing aside the ax, Clay-Boy dashed for the tree. Reaching it, he slid underneath and hunched there panting.

The buck charged blindly, rack down. When he reached the spot where Clay-Boy had been standing he checked his run, jerked his antlered head aloft, breathed in deeply, and searched about for his enemy. Carried on the wind, Clay-Boy's scent betrayed him.

Again the buck lowered his antlers, and with a quick rush he attacked the tree. Clay-Boy could feel the impact at the base of the tree when wood and antlers clashed. For a moment the antlers were enmeshed in the hemlock branches, but with a powerful wrench the deer freed them. Clay-Boy could feel the enraged breath and smell its foul odor and hear the whistle of the wind as the buck slashed at the tree, first with its antlers and then with its slender, wicked hooves.

For a moment the buck withdrew, but only to brace himself for a second assault. The second attack was more powerful than the first. Clay-Boy felt the tree shudder, heard the impact of antler against wood. Then to Clay-Boy's astonishment the rack of antlers simply dropped only a few feet away from his eyes. Already past their normal time to drop, they had simply cracked away from the buck's skull. Shorn of his antlers, the buck backed away in confusion.

The buck's bewilderment was temporary. With renewed rage he attacked the tree with his front hooves, making short loping runs, rearing up and slashing down through the branches. If he continued he would eventually strip every branch from the tree and Clay-Boy would be exposed. There was no place for the boy to run, and it would do no good to call for help because he was alone on the mountain.

Crouched in his rapidly disappearing sanctuary, Clay-Boy searched about for a weapon. He found only the resinous pine knots. He lifted one. It would do for a club, but even as he hefted it Clay-Boy knew it was no match for the slashing hooves.

Once again the deer charged. Looking up, Clay-Boy could see the sweating nose, the strained visible breath, the wild bloodstained eyes. Albinos' eyes were said to be weak and sensitive. Clay-Boy counted on the truth of that folklore.

Plunging his hand into the pocket of his father's jacket, he grasped the box of kitchen matches. His hand trembled as he withdrew a match, and scratched it against the friction board until it lit. Holding the flame against the splintery underside of the pine knot he prayed that the knot would catch fire. One splinter caught flame, and then another and another. A drop of resin sputtered for a moment, then sizzled and added fuel to the fire. It took only one match. Sheltering the

small flame with his jacket, Clay-Boy waited. The
flame grew and in moments the knot was a glowing
torch.

The buck was poised for a new assault on the tree.
He bound forward, raised his hooves and brought
them crashing down through the limbs. At the same
moment, Clay-Boy rose and thrust the flaming torch
toward the buck's face. The deer snorted at the insult,
reared upward, and then bolted away from the tree,
momentarily blinded by the light, crashing through
thickets of persimmon and chinquapin.

At the edge of the wood, the buck stopped and
turned, looked back with crazed eyes as Clay-Boy
emerged from underneath the ragged tree, still holding
his torch aloft.

The doe had nearly succeeded in freeing herself.
Keeping one eye on the buck, who stood pawing the
ground at the edge of the pine wood, Clay-Boy
grasped one large tree limb in the deadfall, gave it one
powerful tug, and the doe leaped free.

Limping slightly she bounded into the forest. The
buck turned and followed.

"Merry Christmas, you hellion!" shouted Clay-Boy,
his voice fading quickly in the insulating snow. Clay-
Boy picked up his ax and looked back at what was to
have been the Christmas Tree. The ground around it
was churned and torn from the buck's onslaught. The

tree itself had been ruined, but Clay-Boy was grateful
for the protection it had afforded him. It would not be
hard to find another. The woods were full of Christmas Trees.

Throwing the ax over his shoulder, Clay-Boy
started back down the slope. Darkness would be upon
the ridges soon, but Clay-Boy walked in a rosy circle
of light cast by the pine knot torch. Even so, he looked
back over his shoulder from time to time.

At the foot of the mountain he found another hemlock, almost as pretty as the first. He chopped it down
and lifted it on his shoulder. Just at that moment, un-
warmed by any sunset light, the grey day darkened
into night. He walked in darkness now, for the resin
torch had burnt out. He did not mind. The lights of
home were within his sight.

THREE

Two applesauce cakes were on display in the middle of the kitchen table when Clay-Boy walked in. He breathed in the spicy aroma appreciatively. Something had happened during his absence. There was some quickening of excitement, a sense of Christmas rushing inexorably down upon them, but in spite of the two proud cakes, he knew that his mother was not really prepared for the day.

"I was getten ready to send out a search party for you," said Olivia. She stood by the old wood-burning cook stove, where she was frying slices of ham.

"I just poked along," lied Clay-Boy. Olivia was inclined to be overly protective, and he had learned not to reveal his more dangerous adventures on the mountain for fear she might not allow him to venture there alone.

"Did you get the tree?" she asked.

"Yes ma'am," he answered. "It's out on the porch. Where is everybody?" asked Clay-Boy, sensing an unnatural quiet in the house.

"I sent the children over to ask Mama and Papa to come have supper with us."

Clay-Boy noticed that the ham had been pared down to the bone and that every edible slice had been removed. He knew that it was the last ham left from the hog his father had butchered and cured in the fall.

"Mama, what are we goen to have for the Christmas dinner?"

"I don't know, boy," answered Olivia. "Maybe I'll wring Gretchen's neck and make stew and dumplins."

"Gretchen's a layen hen," objected Clay-Boy. "What'll we do for eggs if we make a stew out of her?"

"I don't know that either," replied Olivia. "I'm feelen reckless. Liven each day as it comes. Let tomorrow take care of itself."

Olivia tried to make her voice sound convincingly free of care, but she didn't succeed. She and Clay-Boy both knew that the money Clay had left with her last week for food had dwindled to less than three dollars. There were some sweet potatoes left in the storage bin in the basement, some dried apples, and a few Mason jars of canned tomatoes, peas, string beans and peach preserves left from her summer's canning. Seeing

Clay-Boy's troubled look, Olivia said reassuringly, "We'll get by."

"What about Santa Claus for the kids?" he asked.

"I made some little things," answered Olivia. "Dresses for each of the girls. Warm pajamas for you boys."

"They'll know you made them," observed Clay-Boy. "They'll know they're not from Santa Claus. They'll stop believen."

"Maybe it's time they did," said Olivia soberly. "In hard times like these maybe it's silly to let children go on believen in foolishness."

"I remember when I was little," said Clay-Boy. "Remember how we used to put out corn flakes for Santa Claus and carrots for his reindeer? It used to take me hours to get to sleep, thinken of him right here in the house. And then in the mornen when the presents were all under the tree and the corn flakes and carrots all gone, I *really* believed, Mama. I believed."

"Times were different. We had money to spend in them days."

"You reckon the Depression will last forever, Mama?"

"I don't know, boy," answered Olivia wearily. "Mr. Roosevelt says it won't. Now stop worryen about things you can't help. Go put up the Christmas Tree. At least we'll have somethen pretty to look at."

Clay-Boy went to the barn, found his father's hand-saw and a square block of wood to use as the base for the Christmas Tree. He returned to the back porch where the tree leaned against the wall. There he shook the tree vigorously, freeing it of the powdery snow which still clung to its limbs so it would be dry enough to take into the house. He sawed the pungent trunk of the evergreen evenly, and nailed the square block to the foot of the trunk.

The boy worked rapidly to set up the tree in the living room before his brothers and sisters arrived home. They would clamor to start decorating it immediately, and he wanted it ready for them.

Once it stood in a corner the tree released its wintery green aroma, which quickly permeated the living room. A tree in the house brought with it a feeling of mystery. Into the house the tree brought with it the memory of thousands of white-hot summer suns, the long wilderness silence of snow-mantled winters, the crash of thunderous storms, the softness of a new green spring, and all the wild things which had rested in its shade or nestled in its branches. There was something pagan and alien in its presence which pervaded the house.

"You sure that's the same tree we picked out last summer?" asked Olivia when she came in to inspect it.

"No, it's not, Mama," replied Clay-Boy. "Some-then broke some branches on that other one."

Just then there was a great stomping of feet on the back porch, and they knew that the children had arrived home. Olivia rushed to the kitchen door, hoping they might have encountered Clay somewhere along the way, that he would be standing there when she opened the door with Pattie-Cake piggyback on his shoulders and the other children holding his hands and coattails. But there were only the children and their grandparents.

"Merry Christmas, daughter," boomed Homer Italiano in his voice, which was so loud that it lent authority to anything he said, no matter how commonplace it might be.

"Come on in, Papa," cried Olivia. "How are you, Mama?"

"I think I got a crick in my back," replied Ida. Homer's wife was a thin wraith of a woman who, unlike her husband, spoke in a thin near-whisper.

Alone with his wife, Homer was tender and dependent, an indulged child as much as a husband, but when they were in the presence of others he found it necessary to deride Ida's talents and personality.

"That woman is crazy," remarked Homer with a wondering shake of his head.

"Don't listen to him," whispered Ida, unbuttoning her coat.

"What's Mama done now," laughed Olivia, ushering the children out of the cold and into the kitchen.

"Been streaken all over the hills taken orders for the Larkin Company. Old woman like her ought to be home sitten by the fire in a rocken chair 'stead of scooten 'round like a snow plow!"

"I made three dollars," protested Ida. "And that's three dollars we wouldn't have if I hadn't been out taken orders."

It was then that the children spotted the Christmas Tree, and with shrieks of delight they streamed into the living room to admire it. The grandparents came to the door and observed the tree for a moment, then turned back to take seats around the kitchen table.

"Where's Clay, daughter?" asked Homer.

"Somewhere between here and Waynesboro," answered Olivia. "Be here soon, I reckon."

"I wouldn't count on it," observed Ida. "I'll bet you he's down yonder drinken whiskey with those Staples women right this second." Ida was a pillar of the Baptist Church and she lost no opportunity to remind her daughter that she had married a heathen.

"Mama, I won't have you talken about Clay that way," objected Olivia.

"He drinks, don't he?" snapped Ida.

"He *takes* a drink," said Olivia. "There's a difference. And anyway it's Christmas Eve. Clay'll want to be with his family."

"At least he's worken," said Homer. "That's more'n can be said for the rest of us."

Nobody had any reply for this.

"Hard times," said Homer philosophically. Ida nodded absently.

"I was listenen to the radio while ago," continued Homer. "They're doen right smart talken about this New Deal."

"It's what the country needs all right," said Olivia.

"I hear 'em talken about it all the time, but I don't know what it means," said Ida.

"It means we got a man in the White House that's goen to do somethen," announced Homer. "Roosevelt says he's goen to open the banks, get the country moven again, and I believe he'll do it. You heard any of them Fireside Chats of his, daughter?"

"I heard one the other night," replied Olivia. "Talken about the NRA or some such thing."

"There's some that feels the country is goen to the dogs," said Homer. "But I don't pay 'em no heed. I say Roosevelt is goen to keep his word."

"They say *she's* real nice," observed Ida. "Joe Phillips was up there in Washington on the Veterans March. She came out there and shook hands with everybody, tasted the stew and all. Joe said he got up as close to her as I am to you."

"I don't care what they do as long as they get the mill open and Clay can come home to work again," said Olivia.

"Clay ought to be showen up here pretty soon," said Homer.

"I expect him any minute," said Olivia, and she gave her mother a confident look to show that she meant what she said.

In the living room there was a crisis. Clay-Boy had been overseeing the decoration of the Christmas Tree. On the topmost point of the tree he had fixed the silver glass star which had belonged to Grandma Spencer. Then they had placed the store-bought ornaments and ropes of tinsel on the tree, but there were still bare spots. To fill them each of the children had brought down from their rooms decorations they had made themselves.

John had varnished some pine cones with gold paint. Mark had found a heavy antique brass key and had polished it so that it shone with a burnished glow. Shirley had joined circles of construction paper together to form a chain. From a piece of red flannel, Matt had constructed a Santa Claus with black-eyed peas for eyes, a lump of coal for a nose and a long ragged cotton beard. Even though she had made it for Thanksgiving, Pattie-Cake, because she was the baby, had been allowed to hang a crayon-colored, cutout of a turkey. From tinfoil Luke had fashioned several silver bells and when the decorations were all in place the tree had developed a certain helter-skelter style.

The trouble developed when Becky arrived with her decoration—a blue jay's nest containing one speckled grayish-blue egg.

"You can't put that thing on the tree," said Matt. "It's full of mites and that old rotten egg will smell bad."

"You don't know what you're talken about," objected Becky. "This egg is *not* rotten. I blew all the stuff out of it. Inside it's clean as a whistle."

"I don't care," said Matt. "It's still got bird poop on it. Who wants a nasty thing like that on a Christmas Tree?"

"I do," said Becky firmly. "And it's not nasty."

"You're such a crazy, Becky," said Shirley.

"Oh, go paddle your canoe," said Becky airily.

Pretending to ignore her brothers and sisters, Becky reached into the most conspicuous spot on the tree and began arranging the blue jay's nest on a handy fork while she sang the first stanza of "The Little Old Cathedral in the Pines."

"All I've got to say," said Clay-Boy, "is Santa Claus is goen to take one smell of that bird poop and he's goen to head right back up the chimney."

Pattie-Cake began to cry.

"What's the matter with you, cry-baby?" demanded Becky.

"Santa Claus won't come because of you," wept Pattie-Cake.

"Look what you've done *now!*" scolded Shirley. "Made her cry."

Patti-Cake began to cry even more loudly.

"You ought to be ashamed of yourself, Becky," said Matt.

"Oh, you're all a bunch of piss-ants," swore Becky.

"Mama! Mama!" several voices chimed at once.

Olivia appeared at the door, wiping her hands on her apron.

"What's the matter?" she asked.

"Becky made Pattie-Cake cry and she ruined the Christmas Tree with bird poop, and she said a bad word!" cried Shirley, her eyes blinking with indignation.

"You asken for a spanken, girl?" inquired Olivia, fixing Becky with an accusing eye.

Becky refused to reply. She turned her head away, lifted her chin in the air and pretended she was a rich city girl in Charlottesville, wrapped in a full length white mink coat, casually shopping for diamonds at Keller and George. She had looked in the window once and ever since had treasured the fact that her eyes had beheld diamonds.

She was saved from the threatened punishment by the sounds of footsteps, stomping off snow on the back porch.

"There's Daddy," several voices shouted in unison,

and like a school of minnows they flowed into the kitchen and threw open the back door.

Standing on the back porch was Charlie Sneed, Clay's friend and companion in hunting and fishing, woodcutting, drinking and poker-playing. Before the Depression he had worked beside Clay in the machine shop. Since the mill had closed he had become a back-woods Robin Hood, poaching game, some of which he sold in Charlottesville for cash money; the rest he gave to friends or families he knew to be in special need.

Charlie's most imposing feature was a large round belly which he called his "beer keg." Sometimes Charlie held himself erect and the "beer keg" moved above and sometimes flowed over his belt. At other times it simply rested comfortably below his belt. Charlie was given to patting it fondly, like a mother fondling some overgrown blob of a child.

Charlie's face was jolly and round. His eyebrows and his hair were thick curls of reddish blond. When he smiled his brown eyes twinkled. He looked for all the world like a rural Santa Claus on his day off, doing some work around the farm.

"Where's Clay?" asked Charlie as he entered the kitchen and closed the door behind him.

"He's late tonight," said Olivia.

"Hey there, Mr. Homer, Miss Ida. How y'all?" asked Charlie.

"Pretty good for old folks," answered Ida.

"Anybody else around here?" asked Charlie mysteriously.

"Just us," answered Olivia wonderingly.

"Ep Bridges been around tonight?"

Ep Bridges was the local sheriff and game warden, the beefy red-neck descendant of a Hessian deserter and a Siouan squaw. He was ardent in his enforcement of law and order, especially those laws concerning the taking of wild game out of season.

"I saw his truck go by once today," answered Olivia. "But he hasn't been around here."

Now Charlie turned to the children who regarded him curiously.

"Can you kids keep your mouths shut if I let you in on a secret?"

"Sure, Charlie," they answered.

With an air of mystery, but yet taking pleasure in what he was doing, Charlie opened the kitchen door and stepped outside. When he came back in he carried a wild turkey gobbler. It had been shot through the head, and its rich bronze and grey and black wing feathers hung down awkwardly.

"I knew Clay wouldn't have a chance to go hunten this Christmas so I thought he'd appreciate a little meat on the table."

Tears welled in Olivia's eyes. She had worried all day about what she would serve for Christmas dinner.

Now she envisioned the turkey, roasted a rich brown, sitting in the middle of the table in her Blue Willow platter.

"We're much obliged to you, Charlie," said Olivia, taking the turkey from him and carrying it to the sink.

"Don't say a thing about it," said Charlie. "It's my pleasure."

"I thought the hunten season was over," said Ida with a faint air of disapproval.

"It is," said Charlie cheerfully.

"Don't it scare you to break the law on Christmas Eve?"

"No, ma'am, it don't," said Charlie firmly. "Why should people go hungry when there's game aplenty?"

"Seems like a sin though," said Ida. "I don't think I could eat it."

"Well, you're goen to, Mama," said Olivia, "if you come to dinner tomorrow. And you stop worryen Charlie. This turkey is the answer to my prayers. I declare, I think I'll cook it tonight! Won't Clay Spencer be surprised when he walks in that door and finds a Christmas turkey roasten in the oven!"

The storm outside seemed less threatening now. Christmas dinner, if nothing else, was assured. She was in her own house and her children were safe from harm. If only Clay were here she could ignore completely the snow-laden wind which roared in baffled rage at the windows and doors.

FOUR

CLAY-BOY sat on a three-legged stool, while he milked the Guernsey cow, Chance, his head resting lightly in her flanks. When his father went off to Waynesboro to work, among the other chores Clay-Boy had inherited were the morning and evening milking. It wasn't a job he minded. The cow placidly chewed her mash, occasionally giving him a companionable flick of her tail. Once she turned and lowed briefly and examined him with her dark, serious, luminous eyes, thanking him, Clay-Boy supposed, for the extra bucket of mash he had given her, since it was Christmas Eve.

A warm silence hung in the barn, broken only by the swishing sound of the milk as Clay-Boy did his work, using both hands to propel the milk into the bucket. The lantern, hung on a nail behind the boy, cast a yellow circle of light which faded at the edge of the circle to grotesque shadows. The door was closed, for the gusty North wind had brought fresh snow which showed no signs of abating.

Clay-Boy thought of the albino deer and the doe. He wondered where they were now and whether the buck had covered the doe successfully. Late breeding would mean that the fawn would be born past the season next summer, and might not mature enough to survive the winter. He resolved to watch for the fawn when summer came. A baby deer would be almost impossible to find because of the near perfection of its camouflage, but if the new creature took its father's albino coloration, Clay-Boy thought he might have a better chance.

The thought of the two animals mating sent a quick rush of longing through the boy. How simple it must be to come together with the freedom of wilderness creatures.

Clay-Boy had never made love to a girl. Desire and yearning would engulf him at the thought and would remain with him, a persistent ache. At school he would boast to the other boys about his conquests, but the other boys must have been as innocent as he to have believed his lies.

The thought and the deed were equally sinful, and he would pray earnestly to God to relieve him of his wicked thoughts. Each year at the Revival at the

Baptist Church, when the minister would work himself into a tremulous frenzy of salvation, when, in a voice worn to a rasping whisper, he would plead for God to touch the sinners in his congregation, Clay-Boy would sit in rigid terror, knowing that God could see into his mind, knew the ugly lust that was entwined in his brain, and he knew that he was past even God's help, for that Healing Touch fell on all shoulders but his own. He would watch with envy those who were saved go marching off to the Mourners Bench, and he knew without doubt that there was nothing ahead for him but the eternal fires of Hell.

Sometimes to flush the evil from his mind, to bring the solace of pure thought, he would try to envision some person, someone stronger than himself, someone who might serve as a good example.

He brought into his fevered brain the image of Miss Parker, his English teacher, a red-headed spinster, a gifted teacher, whose sole passion in life was for the works of William Shakespeare. Almost immediately his mind cooled and his body relaxed.

When he had finished milking the cow, Clay-Boy gave Chance a slap on the rump, picked up the bucket of foamy milk, and walked back through the whirling dance of snow to the house. Sleet was mixed with the snow now, and it fell into the bucket like miniature meteorites plunging to their death with a hiss in the warm milk.

"Daddy home yet?" he asked Olivia as he walked into the kitchen.

"Not yet," answered Olivia from the kitchen sink, where she was plucking the feathers from the turkey.

He placed the bucket of milk on the kitchen table and strained it into the scalded clean Mason jars Olivia had standing ready.

When this was done, he placed the filled jars in the refrigerator, then turned to join his grandparents and his brothers and sisters, who were in the living room listening to *Fibber McGee and Molly* on the radio.

"Buttermilk's still got to be churned, Clay-Boy," called Olivia.

"Churnen is woman's work, Mama," said Clay-Boy resentfully.

"Work is work, boy," replied Olivia. "I'd do it, but I've got my hands full with this turkey."

"Why can't Becky do it?"

"Because she splashes all over creation. I don't know what's the matter with that child!"

"The matter with her is she's thirteen years old," answered Clay-Boy.

"She'll live through it," smiled Olivia. "I just hope the rest of us do."

Clay-Boy picked up the old earthenware butter churn and carried it by the handles into the living room. Grandma Ida had drifted off to sleep in the wing-backed chair, but Grandpa Homer was leaning toward the radio along with the children waiting for Mister Mayor of Wistful Vista to be admitted to the McGee household.

Clay-Boy inserted the long wooden dasher into the churn and began the steady upward and downward churning that would turn the sour clabber into buttermilk.

"Well, good evening, Mr. Mayor," cried Molly McGee as they heard the sound of a door opening and the booming voice of Hizzonor calling Merry Christmas to one and all.

"I can't hear with you slappen that buttermilk around," said Becky to Clay-Boy.

"Go jump in a lake," Clay-Boy advised Becky.

"Y'all heish," warned Grandpa Homer. "The Mayor's brought somebody with him."

The Mayor had brought Clark Dennis with him, and as Dennis' rich voice began singing "Silent Night" Clay-Boy stopped his churning and Olivia came to the door to listen to the end.

"Hot damn, that man can sing!" exclaimed Grandpa Homer, who slapped his knee sharply with his open palm to emphasize his admiration.

Grandma Ida had wakened briefly during the song, but drifted off to sleep again. Now she came awake with a start when Fibber opened the door to his closet and all its contents spilled forth.

"What's the matter?" gasped Grandma Ida.

"The end of the world done come," shouted Homer, "and you slept right through it!"

"It was just Fibber's closet," murmured Grandma Ida, her eyes lighting on Clay-Boy, who was disgustedly slopping the dasher up and down in the churn. "You want me to do that for you, honey?"

"You want to, Grandma?"

"No, I do not, but I'd a heap rather do it than see you take on so."

Gratefully, Clay-Boy moved the butter churn to a position by his grandmother's chair, and she took up her chore with considerable energy.

Olivia was trussing up the turkey when she heard a knock at the door. She delayed answering the door for a moment, fearing bad news. Clay was late. Had there been an accident? Was someone waiting there to tell her that Clay was hurt or dead? She pushed the turkey away, rose from her seat and, still shadowed by apprehension, crossed and opened the door.

The caller was Birdshot Sprouse, a tall, obliging, not-too-bright boy, no older than Clay-Boy, but already a man. Birdshot got his name from a fight he had with C. C. Harkness over a coon. When each of the boys had claimed the prize after a long midnight scramble through creeks and gullies, C. C. Harkness had settled the matter by unloading his double-barrel 21-gauge shotgun in his friend's general direction. Several of the pellets entered Birdshot's left wrist when he raised his arms to protect his face. Doc Campbell had removed as many of the pellets as he could find. When the wound healed over, Birdshot discovered that some had been left behind. He found too that by clenching and unclenching his fist he could make the little blue dots just beneath the skin move about across the sinews and veins. It was kind of a curiosity and it gave Birdshot a name and made him famous in the community.

Birdshot was the son of Skunk Sprouse who made a slim living as a fur trapper along the Rockfish River where it cascaded through the pass on the other side of Spencer's Mountain. Home to Birdshot was where he laid his head. Sometimes it was at his father's shanty, but more often it was wherever he happened to be when night fell, in some farmer's hayloft or in the back room of the pool hall. Birdshot did odd jobs about the village. He would help slaughter hogs for fifty cents. For a dollar he would hoe corn in the blazing hot sun from dawn to dusk. He had worked often for Clay Spencer, was devoted to him, and he knew that Olivia would feed him if he appeared at mealtime.

"Come on in out of the cold," invited Olivia.

Birdshot stepped just inside the door, closing it behind him. There he waited for further instructions before venturing into the room.

"Merry Christmas, Miss 'Livy," he said with a shy smile.

"You too, Birdshot," replied Olivia. "You had your supper?"

"Yes ma'am. Had me a can of Vienna Sausage and a box of crackers and a bottle of Nehi down at the pool hall." He peered off into the adjoining room. "Where's your boys and girls?"

"They're in there listenen to Fibber and Molly," answered Olivia. "Go on in if you want to."

"I got a surprise for 'em," said Birdshot proudly.

In the woods, or on the river or out in the fields, Birdshot was right at home, but he wasn't too sure how to act inside a house. He didn't seem exactly certain how to get from the kitchen door to the living room. Olivia solved the problem by leading the way.

"Hey, Birdshot," called the children.

"Hey, everybody," said Birdshot. He beamed with the importance of news not yet shared.

"Birdshot says he's got a surprise," said Olivia.

"What's that?" asked Clay-Boy.

"They got a Missionary Box down at the post office. Woman just brought it out from Charlottesville on a truck. Says she's goen to start handen out things just as soon as they get a crowd."

"Let's go!" shouted Becky.

The children shot up from their seats like a covey of quail taking flight.

"Wait a minute!" cried Olivia.

A chorus of groans sounded as the children paused in their headlong dash for the clothes closet.

"You've forgotten somethen," said Olivia.

Mystified, the children paused, trying to think what it was they might have forgotten.

"We don't accept charity in this family," said Olivia.

Groans of despair flooded the room. The disappointment in the children's faces was almost too great for Olivia to bear, but she stood her ground, knowing how greatly Clay disapproved of accepting any handout.

"Aw shoot, 'Livy," scolded her mother, "What wrong can it be in 'em getten a toy or an apple or a candy bar?"

"Clay feels real strong about it. He won't even allow me to take that WPA food the government's handen out."

"There's such a thing as a man being too proud," said Ida, and pursed her lips to show her disapproval.

"There's such a thing as a man providen for his own," said Olivia hotly. "And Clay Spencer does that!"

"I don't see him in evidence nowhere tonight providen for his own," said Ida triumphantly.

"He'll be here," said Olivia emphatically.

Birdshot Sprouse shifted his feet uncertainly. He realized that he had precipitated some family crisis.

He knew no way to relieve it, and had no idea how to extricate himself from it.

"Mama, couldn't we just go down there and watch other people get things from the box?" asked Clay-Boy.

"What fun would that be?" asked Olivia.

"It's somethen to do."

"Isn't it somethen to do sitten here listenen to the radio and waiten for Santa Claus?"

"I'll be goen," said Birdshot, and waited for someone to dismiss him.

"I'll walk along with you," said Clay-Boy. "Get a little fresh air." His statement was a challenge to Olivia. The younger children still had to ask permission, but he had reached the point with his parents where he could state his intentions and sometimes meet with no opposition, usually much to his surprise.

Olivia considered objecting, but the sight of her tall, almost man-son, stopped her. Where had the growth come from so suddenly? It seemed only yesterday he had reached her shoulder. Now he was actually looking down at her.

"Can't we go too, Mama?" asked Shirley. "We won't take anything from the Missionary Box."

"We'll just watch," pleaded Becky earnestly.

"Please, Mama," several voices said.

"Aw," said Homer, "Let 'em go, daughter."

[55]

"Well, as long as your brother's goen," said Olivia, "I don't see what harm it can do to watch."

There was a traffic jam at the clothes closet as the whole brood dived in, and each somehow came out with his own jacket and warm sweater and overshoes and galoshes. Pattie-Cake had to be helped on with her snowsuit, but a system had evolved where each of the older children automatically helped one of the others until the entire group was dressed.

"Don't y'all stay late," called Olivia as the group trooped out of the door. "Hold Pattie-Cake's hand."

With Clay-Boy leading the way and Birdshot carrying Pattie-Cake on his shoulders, the children made their way through a path made by Clay-Boy's tracks. The feathery snow sifted gently into their tracks, obliterating them almost as soon as they were left behind.

There was one street light in the informal square which made up the cluster of buildings where the village business was conducted. The post office, the barber shop and the pool hall sat side by side. Directly across the street was the building called the commissary, which in better days had housed the company-owned general store, as well as the business offices of the company which operated the mill. Railroad tracks led off past the back of the commissary to the gang room, which before the company had closed was filled with light and grinding sound, night and day as the great diamond saws cut the huge blocks of soapstone into manageable slabs.

But this night the gang room and the commissary and the post office were dark and silent. A misty light spilled from the windows of the pool hall, but the frosted windows cut off any view from the outside of the sinful gambling and whiskey-drinking and oathsaying that went on in that wicked place.

Birdshot and Clay-Boy herded their little tribe of Spencer children through the crowd which had gathered around the truck. The grinding poverty of the Depression years had already stamped the older faces with a gaunt grey pallor, but the prospect of a gift, of some slight change from the ordinary, the elusive Christmas Spirit, had animated thin faces and brought hope to defeated eyes. Each newcomer joined the group silently, without any greeting to his neighbor. They were proud and independent people. Accepting any kind of outside help went against their grain, but they had put aside their pride this night so that their children might receive some token of Christmas which they themselves were unable to provide.

Gifts were already being passed out by a small, determinedly cheerful lady in a fur parka, ski pants and Wellington boots. She had discovered the area in the fall when she and her husband had driven along the back-country roads to admire the autumn leaves. Few of the people knew her name. She was called simply the "city lady" by those to whom she had distributed food and clothing on trips she had made following her discovery of the proud and suffering community.

The children, with the exception of the Spencers, formed an orderly line and as each child accepted a gaily wrapped package, the city lady called "Merry Christmas," and gave each child a hug or a pat on the head.

The Spencer children watched, their eyes wide with wonder and envy, as some child would shyly accept a gift, have the wrapping torn from it by the time he returned to his parent, to discover baseball bats and wind-up toys (some that worked and some that only worked a little bit), doll clothes, warm socks, slightly used gloves, handkerchiefs in boxes, sweet-smelling soap, music boxes, hand lotion, sparkling rings, a mechanical duck that quacked and walked, metal bracelets, an alabaster egg, a fire engine, a goldfish bowl containing colored rocks and a turreted castle, and kaleidoscopes which, held up to the single street lamp, turned the scene into the memory of a thousand shattered rainbows.

Bitter looks were exchanged among the Spencer children. More than once Becky started to join the line waiting for toys, but Clay-Boy's stern look restrained her.

"Look!" cried Claude Winston to his father, displaying a pair of used, but still serviceable, ice skates.

"See what I got!" exclaimed Willie Witt, holding up a little red train engine which chuffed smoke and rang a sturdy little tin bell when it was wound.

"*The Bobbsey Twins,*" said Elsie Berman ecstatically, then placed the book inside her coat to keep it from being spoiled by the falling snow.

"Here's one for a big boy," announced the city lady. There being no big boys who had not yet received presents, the lady pointed to Clay-Boy and offered the present. "You?"

"You take it," Clay-Boy urged Birdshot.

Sheepishly, Birdshot moved toward the center of the circle. He muttered something inaudible when the city lady presented him with a large package and called "Merry Christmas."

Birdshot did not know what the package contained, but he felt some need to show his gratitude. In desperation a way occurred to him. Other people had found it entertaining, and besides, he had nothing else to offer. Mutely he raised his left wrist and furiously clenched and unclenched his fist.

The city lady seemed not to understand what was expected of her until Birdshot pointed with the index finger of his right hand to the spot underneath his skin where the bird shot pellets danced their grotesque ballet across sinew and vein.

The city lady appeared for a moment as if she were about to back away, but then she looked out into the crowd where she saw one person indicate his own head with his index finger then slowly revolve the finger.

The city lady herself was possessed of physical abnormality. She was double-jointed, and in reply to Birdshot's traveling pellets, she stuck out her hand and began rapidly revolving her thumb a full three hundred and sixty degrees. In his fascination Birdshot forgot to continue his part of the performance, but continued to stare until the lady brought her own performance to an end, but there in the wet snow, in the cold December night, Birdshot Sprouse experienced a unique kind of communication which he had never felt before with another human being. He had reached out to touch someone and that someone had not turned away, but had reached back.

"Merry Christmas," said the city lady quietly. Birdshot nodded. "I'm beholden to you," he replied, then turned and ran back to the Spencer children.

"Open it," urged Clay-Boy when Birdshot returned to the group, still holding the bulky package, showing it to each of the children in turn with a sheepish grin.

Clumsily, Birdshot tore away the wrapping paper to reveal a rich brown tweed jacket with leather patches at the elbows and buttons of real leather and a soft brown silk lining.

"You take it, Clay-Boy," said Birdshot. "It's too nice for me."

"Put it on and stop being silly," said Clay-Boy.

Birdshot slipped his thin arms and shoulders into the jacket and the transition was almost magical. The boy seemed to stand taller. The long skinny wrists were covered and his normally inexpressive face took on an appearance of intelligence and attractive alertness.

"How you feel?" whispered Clay-Boy.

"Like a dude," Birdshot admitted with a blush, and looked around at the crowd, saw himself reflected in their eyes and found they were looking at him, not as an oddity, but as a man.

It was a night of miracles.

"And here's one marked for a little girl. How about you, dear?" called the city lady, and beckoned to Pattie-Cake.

Spellbound, forgetting her mother's admonition about accepting charity, Pattie-Cake moved toward the bearer of gifts. Clay-Boy reached for her, but she was beyond his grasp.

The other children pressed in against Clay-Boy with urgent whispers.

"What's Daddy goen to say?"

"We won't tell him."

"He'll find out."

"We'll hide it till he's gone back to Waynesboro," Clay-Boy replied.

Pattie-Cake accepted the present, thanked the lady,

then ran back to her brothers and sisters. They crowded around her in a tight little circle to watch her open the rectangular box.

Two small, elegantly shoed doll feet appeared as the box was opened and the tissue paper folded back. Then two pink dimpled knees and the beginning of a crisp white organdy dress. "Oh," and "Oh," murmured Pattie-Cake with each new revelation of the doll until at last the face came into view. She stared down at it for a moment, the delight in her face still shining, and then her cries of joy turned to sobs.

"What's the matter, honey?" asked Becky.

Pattie-Cake held out the doll. Suddenly thrust from an upright to a horizontal position, the doll cried "Mama," and its yellow hair fell away from around the permanently arched eyes to reveal that its face was cracked apart from its hair line to its throat. Some ineffectual attempt had been made to glue the face together again, for little beads of glue had formed along the separate sides of the face, but the repair job had not lasted.

"It's ugly," cried Pattie-Cake, dropping the doll in the snow and burying her face in Clay-Boy's lap.

"I'll fix it, honey," said Clay-Boy comfortingly.

"It's scary," sobbed Pattie-Cake.

The city lady, perplexed, looked out at the children and then called, "What's the matter over there?"

The city lady started toward the group, now knowing the problem, but bent upon making amends. Before she reached them a great feeling of shame swept over Clay-Boy. He felt that he had betrayed his father and brought dishonor to the family. He reached down, scooped Pattie-Cake up in his arms and led the way off toward home. Not one of them looked back to their friends and neighbors who had lowered themselves by accepting something they had not earned.

No one spoke on the way home except for Becky, who cursed aloud to the night and the snow.

"Sons-of-bitches! It's just like Daddy always claims," said Becky bitterly. "Nobody ever gave away anything worth keepen!"

And for once everyone was in complete agreement with Becky.

FIVE

Olivia was feeding wood to the old cooking range. She watched the first red blaze appear, heard the sharp crackle and then a spit of sparks. The wood was dry. It would make a hot flame for roasting the turkey. She had objected mildly when Homer and Ida had left, but now that they were gone it was good to be alone in the house, free of her mother's suggestions that Clay was off playing poker, or drinking whiskey or spending the week's paycheck in sinful ways. She poked the stove wood, and when she was satisfied that the fire was going well, she closed out the bright eye of the fire with a stove lid.

She felt better now that she had a plan. It was a village custom that if the man of the house did not return home at some reasonable hour the oldest child in the family would go looking for him. Olivia had taken some pride that she had never had to send Clay-Boy to look for Clay, but tonight she would sacrifice pride. When the children arrived home she installed the younger ones at the radio in the living room and quietly called Clay-Boy into the kitchen.

"What's the matter, Mama?" asked Clay-Boy, his hands outstretched over the cooking range to catch its warmth.

"I didn't want to say it in front of anybody, but I'm worried about your daddy."

"I expect his bus is late. It's a right snowy night."

"Could be any one of a thousand things. Bus could of slid off the road. Maybe he's already at Hickory Creek and the snow's too thick for him to walk the six miles home. It's a blizzard outside."

"I could go look for him, I reckon," said Clay-Boy. Having thought of it, the boy warmed to the idea. It was better than sitting home waiting.

"I thought maybe if you could find Charlie Sneed. He's got that old truck. You tell him I said to ride you over to Hickory Creek and see if there's any sign of Clay walken."

"Charlie's down at the pool hall, or was. I saw his truck down there a while ago."

"Then you try to catch him. Tell Charlie we'll pay for the gas."

"I'll tell him."

"Don't say anything to the children. I don't want them to worry."

Clay-Boy slipped into his father's old sheepskin

jacket and buttoned it across his chest. The jacket was big on him, and he seemed to disappear somewhere inside it, his thin, freckled face swimming inside the turned-up collar.

"What you goen to wear on your head?" asked Olivia.

"My cap's a little wet, but it'll do," replied Clay-Boy.

"Wait a minute," said Olivia. She disappeared into the bedroom and returned with a package wrapped in white tissue paper and tied with a red ribbon bow.

"This was goen to be your present from Santa Claus," she said. "You're getten it early."

From the package Clay-Boy removed a red woolen cap. Olivia had knitted it herself in the long nights alone in the living room after the children had gone to bed and before sleep caught up with her.

"It's right pretty, Mama," said Clay-Boy gratefully, and placed the cap on his head.

"Pull it down over your ears. I made it plenty long so your ears wouldn't freeze."

Olivia found a long warm scarf and wrapped it around his throat so that with the cap above and the scarf below all that could be seen of Clay-Boy were his eyes.

"And if somebody asks what you're doen out, don't you tell them you're looken for your daddy," admonished Olivia as he looked back in parting.

"Yes, ma'am," answered Clay-Boy. He closed the door behind him and thrust himself into the elements. A hard wind slashed the sleet and snow, almost whipping his breath away for a moment, but the coat and cap and scarf protected him. He felt like a warm old turtle inside his shell.

At the corner where the road turned he looked back at the house, but all that was visible were vague damp patches of light which shone from the windows. He plunged down the road and into darkness, making his way more from memory than any landmark he could find with his eyes.

Charlie Sneed's truck was still parked in front of the pool hall when Clay-Boy staggered up through the blizzard. Underneath the single street light he noticed that Charlie had grown careless, for the tarpaulin which covered the back of the pick-up truck had been left loose and underneath, clearly visible, was the antlered head of the poached deer. Clay-Boy pulled the tarpaulin back in place, climbed the steps to the pool hall and entered.

The room he had come into was called "the Restaurant." It occupied one long quarter of the rectangular building, the remainder of the building being given over to the pool hall. A counter lit by a row of bare electric overhead lights ran the length of the restaurant. Tables with soapstone tops surrounded by chairs of a variety of styles filled the remainder of the room. From the adjoining room came the solid click of pool balls hitting against each other.

Clay-Boy was uncertain of his reception here. There was an unwritten law that no children and no decent woman ever entered the building. It was strictly a man's preserve and a jealously guarded one.

"Hey," said a voice which came from Ike Godsey. Ike appeared from behind the counter where he was lethargically washing glasses in a steaming tub of soapy water. Ike, the bald, round-faced owner, bartender, chef and bouncer combined, looked at Clay-Boy with surprise and displeasure.

"You know I can't serve you, Clay-Boy," complained Ike. "Don't you know better'n that?"

"I know that, Mr. Godsey," answered Clay-Boy, shaking the snow away from his shoulders in showers. "I'm looken for Charlie Sneed."

Ike peered into the adjoining room, his face clouded with disgust. He beckoned to Clay-Boy. Puzzled, Clay-Boy crossed to Ike and leaned across the counter between the jar of pickled pig's feet and the beef jerky to where Ike was beckoning him closer with a wave of his hand.

"Is your daddy home from Waynesboro yet?"

"No sir," answered Clay-Boy, "but we're looken for him any minute."

"I wish he'd get here. Maybe he'd talk sense into Ep Bridges."

"What's Ep done now?"

"Arrested Charlie Sneed for hunten out of season. Got him handcuffed in yonder. Claims he goen to throw him in the jail up in Lovingston."

As sympathetic as he was to Charlie's misfortune, Clay-Boy regretted it for personal reasons. He knew of no one else he could ask for a ride to Hickory Creek, and there was no way now that he could be of help to his father if Clay indeed happened to be walking home from the bus stop.

"My daddy been by here tonight?" asked Clay-Boy.

"Nobody breezed in here but that trash that calls himself the Law."

"I reckon I better get home," said Clay-Boy.

"That's where I'm headen as soon as the Law finishes his pool game," said Ike.

"Night, Mr. Godsey," said Clay-Boy, and started back toward the door past the entrance to the pool room. He had not intended to peer in, but when he did, he stopped full in his tracks at the sight of Charlie, sitting forlornly on the bench he was handcuffed to.

"Lord God, Charlie!" exclaimed Clay-Boy sympathetically.

"You ever see such a messed up situation?" inquired Charlie bitterly.

"How'd it happen?" asked Clay-Boy.

"I run over a calf up yonder on the road a piece.

Throwed him in the back of the truck instead of letten him lay there and go to waste."

"First calf I ever seen had ten-point antlers," laughed Ep Bridges from the pool table where he powdered his cue stick with blue chalk. Ep Bridges was two hundred pounds of malice, a beefy, red-faced man with a spare tire of flesh girdling his middle which also supported a Colt .45 on a webbed holster.

"That's one of Clyde Robbins' calves," insisted Charlie innocently. "I was goen to stop by Clyde's and pay him for the damage first thing in the mornen."

"First thing in the mornen you was goen to fry venison," said Ep. "That's what you was goen to do."

"What's goen to become of that calf, Ep?" asked Charlie righteously.

"I'm goen to grind him up and make venison sausage, once the Judge's seen the evidence," said Ep. He leaned against the pool table, supported the cue stick in his crooked index finger and ran the five-, six-, seven- and eightballs into pockets in quick succession.

"That's where you are, Charlie Sneed," chuckled Ep. "Behind the eightball."

"Ep, be a Christian and let me off," pleaded Charlie. "Christmas ain't no time to throw a man in that Lovingston jail. It's cold and drafty. I'm liable to catch pneumonia and die before mornen. You want it on your conscience I died of pneumonia on Christmas Day?"

"You should of thought about that when you dropped that buck," said Ep, draining the can of the last drop of Coors.

"I run over that calf by accident," Charlie persisted. "He just jumped up in front of the truck. I couldn't stop, came near to skidding off the road as it was."

"Come on, Charlie, let's go to Lovingston," said Ep. He tossed his empty beer can into a trash barrel, crossed to the bench where he had handcuffed his prisoner and unlocked the side which held Charlie to the bench.

"Wait a minute, Ep," said Charlie, and turned to Clay-Boy. "You run home and tell your daddy about the fix I'm in."

"Daddy ain't home yet," said Clay-Boy. "We still setten up for him."

"What boy is this, Charlie?" asked the sheriff.

"He's Clay Spencer's boy," said Charlie.

"Last time I laid eyes on Clay Spencer was when I raided that old colored church. They had a poker game goen out there."

"That's probably where he is right this minute," said Charlie wistfully.

"One thing's sure. You ain't goen to be joinen up with him," said the sheriff, and began leading Charlie toward the door.

"Mr. Bridges," called Clay-Boy.

The sheriff turned and looked back at the boy

curiously. Clay-Boy hesitated. He hated to ask a favor of a man who was taking Charlie Sneed to jail, but he was desperate.

"You'll be goen by the colored church on your way to Lovingston, won't you?"

"Sho'," replied Ep.

"You wouldn't give me a ride, would you?" asked Clay-Boy.

"You figuren to get mixed up with a poker game?" asked Ep wonderingly.

"No, sir," answered Clay-Boy, "I just want to see if my daddy happens to be there."

"I ain't supposed to carry riders," said Ep, considering. "But what the hell! It's Christmas! Come on!"

Clay-Boy followed his father's friend and the sheriff to the sheriff's white Dodge with the words COUNTY SHERIFF painted on the doors in forbidding black lettering. Once Charlie was placed in the caged-off back seat, Clay-Boy climbed into the front seat, positioning his feet between the two six-packs of beer which were stored there.

"I could shore use one of them beers," said Charlie piteously from the back seat.

Ep Bridges pretended not to notice Charlie's thirst as he entered the driver's seat and started the car.

The blizzard had abated somewhat, but the snow still fell heavily, making it difficult for Ep Bridges to find the road, and when he found it to stick to it. There had been no cars in or out of the village, so there were no tracks for him to follow. Coming to some place where there was a question, he would get out of the car, shine his powerful torchlight around until he was sure of the direction he should take, and then take it.

"I feel like a damn zoo monkey," grumbled Charlie Sneed in the caged-off back seat. "How about passen one of them beers back here to wet a man's throat?"

Sometimes Ep Bridges would answer, but more often he would ignore Charlie, his attention focused on the difficult driving, intent on delivering his prisoner to the county seat, and going on to The Old Seminole Trail Inn on Highway 29 for a wide slice of coconut-custard pie and to swap jokes and anything else he had to trade with Hallie Stringfellow, the night girl.

It had crossed his mind to stop at the First Abyssinian Baptist Church and put the fear of God into any poker players who might be there, but the thought of Hallie Stringfellow urged him on, and when he came to the turn-off to the First Abyssinian Baptist Church he paused briefly to let the boy out of the car.

"Why don't you give the boy a ride all the way, Ep?" called Charlie from the back seat.

"That road ain't fitten to drive on even in dry

weather," said Ep. "I'd be mired up to my axle before
I went a hundred feet."

"I can make it, Mr. Bridges," said Clay-Boy. "I'm
much obliged for the lift."

"You tell your daddy to come go my bail," called
Charlie just before Ep Bridges reached over, slammed
the door shut and moved off down the road.

Watching the glow of Ep Bridges' headlights
swiftly disappear into the soft sibilant snow, Clay-Boy
wished he had brought a flashlight. The First Abyssinian Baptist Church was a quarter of a mile down an
unpaved road; the snow was already nearly a foot
deep and he had no light to guide him. Blindly, Clay-
Boy started down the road, sometimes losing his way,
knowing he had drifted too far to the right or to the
left when he came to a ditch or to snow-shrouded
bushes. Once he thought he was lost, for he went a long
way with nothing to bar his passage. He thought he
might have wandered into an open meadow, but his
hand touched something, and when he felt it he recognized barbed wire. Clinging to the barbed wire he
continued on, hoping that it would lead him to the
Negro church and not away from it.

SIX

SOMEWHERE, above the screaming wind and the biting whine of snow, Clay-Boy heard singing voices. The voices came and went, then drifted back again, but Clay-Boy made out enough of the words to recognize "It Came upon a Midnight Clear."

Dimly ahead of him he saw a light, and he let go of the barbed-wire fence which he had clung to like a life line, and plowed through the snow toward the square of light. The voices grew stronger, and by the time he came to the graveyard behind the church, Clay-Boy knew that no white men were playing a clandestine game of poker in the church tonight. The rightful tenants had occupied it, and a service was in progress.

Clay-Boy entered the vestibule, which was separated from the main church room by folding doors. He had intended to rest there for a moment and warm himself, but as he opened the outer door the wind forced the folding doors open and row after row of startled dark faces turned to see who had entered. Now the swinging doors folded shut again, and Clay-Boy debated what to do. If he went in he would interrupt the service; if he remained where he was the people might think he was some white man there on mischief. The singing voices had already died away. He realized that by standing there he was already increasing the worshipers' anger or anxiety or whatever they might be feeling, so he pushed the swinging doors aside and went in.

Row after row of black faces looked back at him questioningly. He stood there for a moment, uncomfortable that he had interrupted the service, seeing in the eyes that gazed at him that he had no right there and was not welcome. A wave of resentment flowed through the congregation, a murmur of whispered voices melting toward anger. He wanted to speak, to tell them that he was not one of the white men who desecrated their church with their poker playing, but he could not find the words to say it.

"Is that you, Clay-Boy?"

The speaker was a man standing at the foot of the center aisle. He was a man in his fifties, a vigorous, muscular, tall man whose hair was just beginning to be touched with grey. Because the man was dressed in a black suit, white shirt and black tie, Clay-Boy had not recognized Hawthorne Dooly, a farmer whose land Clay-Boy and his father had often gone to to hunt and fish, a leader in the Negro community.

"Hey, Hawthorne," said Clay-Boy.

"What you doen out here?"

"I was lost," said Clay-Boy.

"Come on down here and warm yourself," said Hawthorne.

"I don't want to get in the way," said Clay-Boy.

"Come on up to the fire," said Hawthorne and met Clay-Boy halfway down the aisle of wooden benches, and led him to where the pot-bellied stove glowed red and hot. Clay-Boy was conscious of the watching eyes turning from resentment to acceptance, and he was relieved.

"Scrunch over," Hawthorne called to a family on the bench nearest the fire. Obliging, smiling now that he was a welcome guest, the family moved together to make room for Clay-Boy at the end of the bench.

Clay-Boy was reassured by the smiles of the two little boys sitting next to him. He had never been anywhere where he was the only white person present, and it made him nervous. He had been told things about Negroes, told that they were different from white people. Wondering how they worshiped God, he guessed maybe they might sing spirituals or roll on the floor like Holy Rollers.

Hawthorne returned to his position in front of

the congregation, looked out over his flock and announced, "We'll continue the service with hymn number three hundred and two."

There was a rustling of pages as hands turned the pages of hymnals, found the page, and waited. Now Hawthorne led off with the first line of the hymn and the congregation joined in.

> *O little town of Bethlehem*
> *How still we see thee lie,*
> *Above thy deep and dreamless sleep*
> *The silent stars go by.*

Clay-Boy felt something nudge his elbow and he looked down to see that the little boy standing next to him was offering to share his hymnal. Clay-Boy knew the words, but he smiled back at the little boy and pretended to sing from the book, joining his voice to the richness of the old Christmas hymn.

> *Still in thy dark night shineth*
> *The everlasting light,*
> *The hopes and fears of all the years*
> *Are met in Thee tonight.*

The song reached its end and silence fell in the room. Hawthorne tiptoed to the side of the center

platform and pulled a clothesline on which sheets had
been hung to form a curtain. As the curtain parted
there came into view a barnyard setting. Instruments
of work, a hoe, a scythe, a pitchfork hung from a
wooden backdrop. In front of the backdrop two sheep
and a goat were lying quietly beside an old wooden
cradle. Two roosters pecked at corn and walked as
far as the cord tethers allowed.

When the curtain had parted, Hawthorne picked
up his Bible and began to read:

*And it came to pass in those days, that there went
out a decree from Caesar Augustus, that all the world
should be taxed. And all went to be taxed, each one
into his own city.*

Two figures appeared from behind the backdrop
and made their way down the platform to the sheep
and goats and chickens. Clay-Boy recognized the little
black Joseph as Hawthorne's grandson, Claudie. He
wore a flowing purple velvet cape, and a turban of the
same material was wound about his head. Following
Claudie was little Emmarine Hoover, the daughter of
Estelle Hoover who taught the one-room Negro
school. As Mary, Mother of Jesus, she was clad in a
white tunic and on her head was a glowing silver halo.
The children reached the wooden cradle, stole a fur-

tive look out toward the congregation, then knelt in practiced unison.

"And so it was," read Hawthorne, "that while they were there, the days were accomplished that she should be delivered."

Mary reached into the cradle and picked up a doll. She held it to her breast for a moment then offered it for Joseph's inspection. Now, casually, almost conversationally, Joseph began to sing:

> *Hey, Mary, what you goen to name*
> *That pretty little baby?*

And Mary answered:

> *Some call him one thing,*
> *I think I'll call him Jesus.*

"Oh yes," cried affirming voices in the congregation.

Behind the children appeared other children, dressed as shepherds and wise men, and they repeated the query:

> *Hey, Mary, what you goen to name*
> *That pretty little baby?*

And once again, Mary replied:

*Some call him one thing,
I think I'll call him Emanuel!*

"Yes, Lord," said voices in the congregation. And now the men took up the question Joseph had asked, and the women answered along with Mary, and their voices rose and the pace quickened until they could no longer sing from their seats, but had to rise and shout for Glory and exaltation at the coming of the Lord. Reverently, the singing voices lowered almost to a whisper. Onstage, the shepherds and wise men approached the Child and knelt with bowed heads.

Now a powerful voice, controlled, tremulous, reverent, began to sing, and when Clay-Boy looked he saw that it was Hawthorne, his face lifted to Heaven, his eyes closed.

*"O holy night! The stars are brightly shining,
It is the night of the dear Savior's birth.
Long lay the world in sin and error pining
Till He appear'd and the soul felt its worth.*

Shivers went down Clay-Boy's back. He had heard the hymn since he was a baby, carried to church in his mother's arms, but he had never heard it sung this way before. Hawthorne crooned the song, stroked and caressed it with tenderness, letting his voice cling to the melody, elongating the last line as if reluctant to let it go, until the feeling and the events the song described seemed to be taking place now and here and not two thousand years ago in some distant Biblical storybook place.

A thrill of hope the weary world rejoices,
For yonder breaks a new and glorious morn.
Fall on your knees! O hear the angel voices!
O night divine! O night when Christ was born!
O night divine! O night, O night divine.

The song ended; the congregation in a single voice spoke, "Glory Hallelujah!"

Hawthorne bowed his head, and the congregation followed suit.

"We thank Thee Father for the Gift of Thy Son. Help us to be worthy of Thy sacrifice, and to walk in Thy light all the days of our lives. Amen."

"Amen," answered the congregation.

Hawthorne Dooly glanced toward the rear of the church and nodded a signal.

"Ho-Ho-Ho!" came a booming voice from the vestibule. Every head turned and the children's eyes widened with awe as a roly-poly Santa Claus came marching up the aisle.

"Merry Christmas! Merrrry Christmas!" he called as he stopped to shake hands with a grownup or pinch some youngster's cheek.

To each child he passed out an orange, and when he came abreast of Clay-Boy and offered him an orange too, Clay-Boy remembered how his father felt about accepting charity, but at the same time he did not want to hurt the black Santa's feelings, and accepted the gift from the outstretched hand.

Carrying his orange, Clay-Boy started for the door while families rose and visited with each other and waited for each child to receive his gift.

As he made his way past the Negro faces it came to him that he did not really know any Negroes. He knew those in the village, but he had never been in one of their homes and did not know what they yearned for or what their dreams were. He felt a sense of loss that an entire community existed within the larger community and he did not know one of them beyond his name and face.

When he reached the door, Hawthorne Dooly was waiting for him.

"You out this way looken for your daddy?" asked Hawthorne.

"I reckon so," answered Clay-Boy.

"Have you tried the Staples place?"

"No, I didn't. So far out there."

"It ain't all that far if you've got transportation,"

said Hawthorne. "You come and ride on General with me."

Gratefully Clay-Boy accepted the offer and a short while later was riding through the silver night on a white horse with a black man guiding the way. Once the snow lifted. The moon shone sulkily through scudding clouds. Clay-Boy could see their shadow moving along with them in the glittering luster which blanketed the world. We could be two of the wise men, hurrying after some bright star, thought Clay-Boy.

SEVEN

In observance of Christmas Eve, Miss Emma and Miss Etta Staples had gotten out of the overalls they usually wore, and changed into finery. It was Emma's idea. Etta was a ninny and never had an idea of her own. It would have been just like her to have forgotten Christmas altogether and worked right through to New Year's. But Emma remembered and it was she who cut the tree and set it up, laid the fire in the seldom-used front room, then briskly climbed the stairs to change.

"Hurry along, Etta," called Emma, passing her sister's door, knowing full well that Etta was such a dreamer that she might lose herself in a magazine and forget why she had come to her room altogether.

"I'm almost ready," Etta called gaily from behind the closed door.

"Wait for me," called Emma. "We'll go down together."

Quickly Emma changed into her good dress, a plain black wool which she had bought in Charlottesville for Papa's funeral. There had been lace at the collar, but Emma did not care for lace and had removed it. Stopping at the dresser, she picked up the cameo brooch which had been her mother's, stuck it in the front of the dress, then touched her hair with a comb. Hair was a nuisance most of the time. Emma cut her own, kept it short and clean, and observed with a twinge that there was more grey present than the last time she had looked. Emma gave her hair one final whack, lay down the comb and left the room.

Hearing Emma's door open, Etta opened her own door and self-consciously walked out into the hall.

"My, Etta!" exclaimed Emma. "You could win a beauty contest!"

Etta had taken some pains with herself and she did indeed look beautiful. Her hair had turned pure white, with none of the yellow which streaked her sister's. She had combed it straight back and put it into a bun, and it framed her small well-made face like a halo. At her throat was a black velvet choker, and the dress she wore was a lavender silk.

"You look nice, too," said Etta, observing the cameo brooch her sister wore. She had wondered where the brooch had gotten off to. She planned to steal it back when the first opportunity arose. She fancied that Emma was constantly stealing her things, and she resolved to hide the brooch better once it was back in her possession.

"Where are the decorations, Emma?" asked Etta at the head of the stairway.

"They're already by the tree, just waiting for you to put them up," replied Emma.

"I feel just like when we were little," said Etta happily as they walked into the front room and she saw for the first time the tree which Emma had set up earlier in the day.

Etta opened the box of decorations and was swept into yesterday. Emma watched, taking pleasure in their yearly visit with the decorations they had known since they were children. Out of the box and onto the tree went doves made of spun glass, angels with wings of gauze, ropes of glass beads, a dozen little tin trumpets, stars of gold, and glass bells with glass clappers, a hand-carved Santa Claus and all eight reindeer.

While Etta worked at the tree, Emma arranged the crèche on the old walnut end-table beside the horsehair sofa. She had placed the Jesus figure in the manger and was reaching for a lamb, when there came a knocking at the front door.

"Someone has run out of Recipe!" said Etta.

"I was sure everybody had laid in a good supply," said Emma and opened the door.

"Who is it?" asked Emma doubtfully, observing the snow-covered figure just beyond the door.

"Clay-Boy Spencer," answered the boy through lips that were numb with cold.

"What a treat!" cried Miss Emma. "Company, Etta!" she called gaily over her shoulder. "It's Clay Spencer's son. Come in! Come in!"

Showers of snow fell away as Clay-Boy removed his cap and scarf, then shook his coat and stamped his feet.

"Why, you're just caked with snow!" said Miss Etta, taking his jacket and hanging it on the clothes rack.

"You look frozen to death," cried Miss Emma. "Come by the fire and warm yourself."

Clay-Boy had been in the kitchen of the Staples' house, but he had never seen the front room. It was grand beyond his imagining. Tasseled lamps rested on heavy hand-carved tables. Two horsehair love seats flanked the fireplace. In a corner an ancient grandfather's clock was stopped at twelve minutes past two, and Miss Etta beamed at him from beside a Christmas Tree which shimmered with all manner of glowing, shining, many-colored ornaments.

"Etta, this boy is frozen through and through. Take off your shoes, Clay-Boy, and let them dry while you visit. Etta, bring some eggnog and put some Recipe in it."

"Don't go to any trouble," said Clay-Boy, but Miss

Etta was already on her way to bring the eggnog. "I can't stay but a minute."

"Nonsense," said Miss Emma. "Take off those wet shoes before you come down with lung trouble. The socks, too. They're soaking wet."

"It's a wonder you haven't got frostbite," said Miss Emma when Clay-Boy's feet, blue with cold, were exposed. "You sit down and wait right here."

Now Miss Emma left the room also and Clay-Boy sat down on the love seat and held his feet out toward the warmth of the fireplace. He felt silly, but he was grateful as the numbing cold began to seep out of his fingers and toes.

Miss Emma and Miss Etta returned together. Miss Emma carried a large steaming pan of water which she placed at his feet.

"Soak your feet in this hot water," she commanded. "It will ward off lung disease."

Obediently Clay-Boy placed his feet in the pan, feeling sillier by the minute, but knowing it was useless to argue with the two old ladies.

"Doesn't that feel better now?" asked Miss Emma.

"Yes, ma'am," he answered.

Now Miss Etta came forward carrying a tray on which she had arranged a silver pitcher and three silver mugs.

"This will warm you up," she promised. Clay-Boy

accepted one of the mugs, which was filled with eggnog lightly sprinkled with cinnamon. Something in
it warmed him all the way to the pit of his stomach,
and once it rested there, radiated throughout the rest
of his body. Miss Emma and Miss Etta waited expect-
antly for some reaction from him.

"It's powerful good," said Clay-Boy. "What's in
it?"

"It's Papa's Recipe," explained Miss Emma. "Papa
used to make it all the time and then when he passed
on we used to get so many calls for it that Sister and I
just kept on making it. Drink hearty. There's plenty."

"We had a gentleman stop in last week all the way
from Warrenton, Virginia," said Miss Etta. "He loved
it so he took a whole gallon back home with him."

"It gives us something to do in our old age," said
Miss Emma, "and it makes people happy, so I can't
see why we shouldn't keep right on providing. Etta,
help Clay-Boy to another cup of eggnog."

Miss Etta poured, and Clay-Boy accepted the refilled cup gratefully. He was warm now from head to
toe and he was beginning to feel so lightheaded and
relaxed that it seemed the most natural thing in the
world to be sitting with the two antique ladies, sipping
eggnog while his feet soaked in a pan of hot water.

"How are your mother and all those dear children?"
inquired Miss Etta.

"Everybody's just fine," said Clay-Boy between sips of the warming eggnog.

"There are eight now, I believe," said Miss Etta.

"Yes, ma'am," replied Clay-Boy. "Last time we counted it was eight."

"Your father never comes but what he says for us to come over and visit," observed Miss Emma, "but we never seem to get out any more."

"We're getting old," said Miss Etta proudly. "Hard to get around when you're old."

"Your daddy says you make good grades at school," said Miss Emma, looking at Clay-Boy appraisingly.

"Yes, ma'am."

"What are you going to do with your life?"

"I don't know yet."

"What do you want to do with it?"

"They seem to think real high of Daddy over where he works. He says they'll put me on over there if I learn a trade."

"Are you interested in taking up a trade?"

"None that I know of. Maybe I'll find somethen," said Clay-Boy.

"If you had your choice, what would you be?"

Clay-Boy had never confessed his secret yearning to anyone in the world before, but the eggnog while warming him had also released his inhibitions.

"You know these Big Five tablets?" he asked. "Like you do homework in?"

Miss Emma nodded interestedly.

"I keep one under my mattress."

"You're just like Etta," said Miss Emma. "She hides things under her mattress too."

"Just letters from my beaux," said Miss Etta, then turned accusingly to her sister. "And now that I know you've been snooping I'm going to hide them somewhere else."

"Her beaux!" cried Miss Emma derisively. "Way she tells it you'd think she had a regular Hallelujah Chorus lined up at the gate."

"I wonder what ever happened to Ashley Longworth," sighed Miss Etta.

"Papa chased him off is what happened," Miss Emma reminded her.

Miss Etta said wistfully: "Once when we were in Charlottesville we were walking along and I thought I saw him, the back of his head, walking along in front of me. I nearly ran, trying to catch up with him, but when I did, the man was a stranger. He could never have been Ashley Longworth. Ashley had fine features. He came from a good family, and he was a gentleman. Emma, why didn't Papa like him?"

"I don't remember any more," said Emma. "Nobody was ever good enough for Papa."

"I never told you this, Emma," said Miss Etta, "but Ashley Longworth kissed me one time."

"If you've told me once you've told me a thousand times," sighed Miss Emma.

"He was a student, you see," Miss Etta continued, ignoring her sister's bored expression, "over at the University. He liked hunting and fishing, and somehow found his way out here, and asked permission to hunt on Papa's land. Papa said yes, and Ashley just got to be a regular fixture out here every weekend. Wasn't he a handsome thing, Emma?"

"Knew it, too," commented Emma from her chair where she sipped her eggnog reflectively.

"Anything that handsome had to know it," Miss Etta commented and turned back to Clay-Boy. "On my twenty-fifth birthday, October 19, 1902, Ashley was here as usual and he asked me to go for a walk with him. The woods were on fire with color, and we stopped beneath a maple tree that had turned blood-red. There was a little breeze and a shower of leaves fell around us. Ashley reached up very impulsively and touched my cheek and that was when he kissed me."

"Having no idea that Papa was standing a hundred feet away," said Miss Emma.

"Papa was very upset about it all. Ashley left that evening and I heard from him once, a farewell letter, you might call it, and then nothing. I think of him often, but as the years went by and no more word of him came, I decided he must have died in one of the wars."

Clay-Boy shook his head sympathetically as Miss Etta turned away and gazed thoughtfully at the Christmas Tree.

"Ah me!" said Miss Emma to no one in particular and, for a while, each of them was alone with his separate thoughts.

"Etta, put a record on the Victrola," said Miss Emma. Etta had been sitting looking dreamily at the Christmas Tree, and did not hear. "Etta!" called Miss Emma sternly.

Miss Etta rose and floated to the Victrola. She searched about in the storage cabinet beneath the machine, found a record and placed it on the turntable.

"It probably needs winding," advised Miss Emma. "It hasn't been used since the last time we had a party."

"That was before Papa died," said Miss Etta as she cranked the handle of the Victrola. "Remember his cousins from Buckingham County dropped in; he hadn't seen them in years. He brought them all in here and we played hymns and sang and afterward everybody cried and hugged."

"Papa was a rounder," said Miss Emma reflectively. She refilled her silver mug with eggnog and then, noting that Clay-Boy's mug was empty, filled his, too.

Miss Etta moved the lever which turned on the

Victrola, placed the needle in the groove, and stood with hands folded while the machine made a couple of preliminary scratchy revolutions.

Then music came into the room and the two old women and the boy listened silently as Enrico Caruso sang "It Came upon a Midnight Clear."

For a moment when the song was over, they remained still.

"The nice thing about life," said Miss Etta, "is you never know when there's going to be a party."

"It wouldn't of been if Clay-Boy Spencer hadn't taken it in mind to stop in," said Miss Emma.

When Clay-Boy realized that they thought the object of his trip had been to pay a call, he decided not to tell them otherwise. His father was obviously not there, nor had he been there, for the old ladies would surely have mentioned it.

But now when he looked there were four old ladies, a twin Miss Emma and a twin Miss Etta, their images blurring and wavering into each other. His lips and his tongue were edged with numbness, and he would have liked nothing better than to have stretched out and gone to sleep.

He roused himself and with some difficulty managed to stand upright, although the rest of the room swam unsteadily.

"I certainly appreciate everything," he said in the general direction of his hostesses.

"Oh, you mustn't go yet," cried Miss Etta. "It's still the shank of the evening!"

"No, ma'am, I expect it's getten along toward eleven o'clock."

"How are you traveling, Clay-Boy?" asked Miss Emma.

"On foot, ma'am," he replied.

"Why, you'll never get home walken in this weather," said Miss Etta, "unless Santa Claus comes along and gives you a lift."

"It's a bad night out there, Clay-Boy," said Miss Emma. "Why don't you stay here? We'll make you comfortable."

"I appreciate it, but my folks would worry."

Suddenly Miss Etta rose and crossed to her sister and whispered something in her ear. She looked back to Clay-Boy briefly. "Excuse my bad manners," she said, and then the two ladies held a brief whispered conference.

At the end of it, Miss Emma rose, fixed an eye on Clay-Boy and said, "Wait here."

When her sister left the room, Miss Etta gazed at Clay-Boy with a sweet smile and said, "We've arranged a little surprise for you."

Clay-Boy looked worriedly after Miss Emma as he heard a door slam at the back of the house.

"I really ought to be getten home."

"Oh, you'll be home before you know it," said Miss Etta. "Now get into your things while I get the blankets!"

Clay-Boy felt he had fallen into the clutches of two old Christmas witches and he was tempted to slip out of the front door before either of them returned with whatever insane plan they had for getting him home.

He felt his socks, which had been hanging by the fireplace and, grateful that they were almost dry, he slipped them on. His shoes were stiff from having dried so close to the fire, but he slipped them on his feet and was lacing them up when Miss Etta appeared at the foot of the stairway. She had put on an old fur coat with a hat to match and she carried several lap robes in her arms.

"Wouldn't you like one more eggnog?" she called. "A small one for the road?"

"I had just enough," said Clay-Boy.

"It does make you feel good, doesn't it?" said Miss Etta gaily.

"Yes, ma'am," replied Clay-Boy who could hardly feel anything at all.

From somewhere outside the house came the silver jingle of bells.

"There she is!" cried Miss Etta, grabbing up the pile of blankets. "Come!" she called and rushed toward the front door.

[97]

Clay-Boy drew in his breath at the magic landscape beyond the door. The snow had stopped and the sky was a deep blue without a cloud in sight. A full moon shone down on an expanse of virgin snow, and waiting in the driveway was Miss Emma Staples in a horse-drawn sleigh.

"It's Papa's sleigh," explained Miss Etta. "We've kept it dusted and polished all these years. Just waiting for an occasion!"

"Hurry up before Lady Esther falls asleep again," called Miss Emma. Lady Esther, an old black mare, was the only one who showed no enthusiasm for the journey.

Clay-Boy helped Miss Etta into the sleigh, then climbed in after her.

"Gee hup!" called Miss Emma while Miss Etta arranged blankets over everybody's knees.

Lady Esther moved forward through the snow, and once she discovered the ease with which the sleigh flowed gently behind her, she seemed to warm to her job and broke into a lively canter.

"Oh my!" exclaimed Miss Etta as each turning of the road revealed a new white landscape that glittered and sparkled in the moonlight.

"What a treat!" exclaimed Miss Emma as she listened to the merrily jingling bells pealing out across the still night.

Oh, God, thought Clay-Boy. Good manners decreed that he should ask the two old sisters in when they arrived at his home. Mama would hit the roof!

EIGHT

THE children had been sitting drowsily around the living room table, but when they heard the sounds of sleigh bells they jumped up with cries of astonishment.

"It's Santa Claus!"

Even Olivia rushed to the living room window and brushed aside the curtains to look down at the front gate. There clearly in the cold white light was a sleigh, drawn by a horse which stamped its hooves and blew clouds of vapor into the air. Someone detached himself from the sleigh, stood for a moment and waved. "Merry Christmas," came the words across the yard, and then the horse turned smartly and drew the sleigh away from the gate and it was lost at the turning of the road in a diminishing silver rattle of sleigh bells.

"It's Clay-Boy," said Olivia, as the figure turned and walked up the front walk. Her heart went cold with disappointment. He had not found his father, and the time was racing toward midnight. Fear for Clay, and anger with him too, rose in her throat. Where could he be? Why wasn't he home with the family on this of all nights?

She followed the children to the kitchen and waited there until Clay-Boy opened the door and entered. He looked to Olivia questioningly and she shook her head. The children caught the exchange, sensed what it implied, and fell silent.

The roasted turkey, still warm from the oven, rested in the center of the table beside the two applesauce cakes, but the joy was gone from them now. They had been the trappings of a festival. Now they were simply food.

"Who was that let you off at the gate?" asked Olivia.

"It was Miss Emma and Miss Etta," said Clay-Boy holding out a Mason jar of Recipe. "They sent this. Said it was Christmas Cheer."

"It's bootleg whiskey is what it is," observed Olivia.

"What do you want me to do with it, Mama?"

"I'll take it," said Olivia, accepting the jar. "I can use some to make frosting for my applesauce cakes."

Clay-Boy looked around at the children, who were still not in their pajamas.

"Shouldn't you tadpoles be in bed?" he asked.

"I promised them they could go to the stable," said Olivia. "They've been waiten for you."

"Will you go with us, Clay-Boy?" asked Pattie-Cake.

"Sure, honey. I'll go."

"Tell me about it again, Clay-Boy," urged Pattie-Cake.

"Well, a long time ago when Jesus was born it was in a stable, because they didn't have any room at the hotel. Right away, this star as bright as the sun came up in the sky and set over the stable to show the wise men and the shepherds and the angels where the baby Jesus was. The first things to lay eyes on Him except for His Mama and Daddy were the sheep and the horses and the cows and the goats that lived there. Here they were, just dumb old animals that lived in a stable, but they were the first to see Jesus' face."

"Was there a mouse there too, Clay-Boy, like in our stable?"

"I expect so, honey, and maybe some doves and sparrows roosten in the eves. Anyway, ever since that night, animals all over the world wait up, and right at the stroke of midnight, they kneel down and pray and speak in human voices."

"I wonder what they say?"

"Let's go to the barn and find out."

While the children were getting into their warm

clothing, Olivia filled the stove with fresh firewood. She felt near tears and she did not want Clay-Boy to see. He watched her in silence from the door, and finally he said, "Come on, Mama. Why don't you go with us?"

Olivia had heard the legend all her life, had even believed it as a child. When had she stopped believing? Where, along the way, had her belief in miracles left her? For a moment some vestige of that childhood faith returned. Who was there to say that the legend was false?

"I'll go," she said, and took her green corduroy coat from its hanger and was putting it on when the children returned, delighted to have their mother's company for the trip to the stable.

With Clay-Boy leading the way, Olivia watched her brood make their way up through the backyard, past the crab-apple tree to the stable. From Clay-Boy down to Pattie-Cake their shadows made a stairstep pattern in the snow.

Children are such fragile things, she thought. Arrows shot from her body, gone now beyond any calling back. She catalogued them in her mind. Clay-Boy, so smart and ambitious. Becky, so independent, so capable and vulnerable. Shirley, so beautiful and so maternal. Matt, so self-reliant and full of love and promise. John, with the talent born in his hands to

play music on a piano. Mark, all business one minute
and wanting a hug in the next. Luke, the handsome
wild one with his eye already on some far horizon,
and Pattie-Cake, too spoiled to turn her hand for herself, too pretty and sweet to spank. What will become
of them all, God only knows. Life be good to them.
God, help us all.

At the barn, Clay-Boy turned and with his finger
to his lips motioned for silence. He indicated that they
were to use the outside ladder lest their presence become known to Chance and she refuse to pray.

One after another the children furtively climbed
the outside ladder, crept through the sweet-smelling
hay to the edge of the loft and looked down. Olivia
was the last one up. She arranged herself in the hay
and then looked with pleasure at the sight of eight
excited faces peering down where Chance was lit by
the moonlight through cracks in the wall of the barn.

An expectant hush filled the hayloft. The children
breathed lightly. Down below, Chance was standing,
the great bellows of her lungs moving evenly as she
chewed her cud, then reached with her long raspy
tongue into the feed trough for remnants of the mash
Clay-Boy had fed her for supper.

Olivia felt a hand reach into hers and she shifted
her body so that Pattie-Cake might move closer.
Pattie-Cake was trembling and her breath was coming

in an open-mouthed gasp. Whether she was cold or frightened, Olivia didn't know, but she put her arm around her to comfort her.

And then across the hills came the deep bong, bong, bong, of the bell in the steeple of the Baptist church. Old Mr. Higgenbottem always waited there to ring the bell at the stroke of midnight and let the world know that Christmas had come again.

Now the children leaned forward and watched Chance intently. Something quivered in her shoulder, some incentive to movement, and then she folded the ankles and arms of her front legs and went down on her knees, and a human voice spoke.

"I'm a-scared," cried Pattie-Cake, but still the children watched. Chance rested on her knees for only a fraction of a second, then lowered the hind part of her massive body to a reclining position.

The children released the breath they had been holding, and every eye went accusingly to Pattie-Cake.

"You ruined it!" cried Becky.

"I want to go home," cried Pattie-Cake through chattering teeth.

"Just when Chance was goen to speak," muttered Shirley with disappointment.

"There's no truth in it," said Olivia. "It's just a story."

"Mama, Chance was on her knees," objected Becky. "If Pattie-Cake hadn't opened her yap, it would of happened."

Pattie-Cake, cold and frightened, began to sob.

"Come on, Clay-Boy, let's get these children to bed," called Olivia.

Herding the children back to the house, Olivia wished she had not allowed them to go to the barn. Just before she closed the door she looked for one long instant up and down the road, but it was white and cold and empty. Clay Spencer was not on it. Foolishness, she thought. There are no such things as miracles.

NINE

OLIVIA and Clay-Boy sat in the living room. Olivia had brought the wind-up kitchen alarm clock out with her and it sat on the table beside her chair, where its ticking seemed to fill the room.

Olivia had been drowsing, but now when she woke and saw that it was one o'clock, she called softly, "Clay-Boy."

"Hum?" he asked sleepily.

"You go on to bed now."

"I'll wait a little while longer, Mama."

"No, you're sitten there half asleep. Just go on up-stairs and lay down."

"Where you reckon he is, Mama?"

"I don't know any more than you do, son."

"I'll go up and lay down, but I'll keep my clothes on, just in case any word comes."

"I don't expect to hear a word before mornen," said Olivia.

"Good night, Mama," he said at the landing.

"Good night, son."

He was about to call "Merry Christmas," but it was obviously going to be anything but merry so he held his tongue. Tiptoeing, carefully, picking his way around boards that squeaked he made his way to the top of the stairs.

"What time is it, Clay-Boy?" called Becky in a whisper as he passed the room the girls slept in.

"Time for you to be asleep," he whispered, and continued on down the hall to the boys' room.

His brothers, two in each bed, were asleep. Luke had kicked his covers off, so Clay-Boy pulled the blankets and the homemade quilt up and tucked it around Luke's shoulders.

Clay-Boy was starting for his own bed when there came an enormous crash on the roof. At the same moment from somewhere in the backyard someone could be heard shouting and cursing. Again the thudding noise came on the roof and in the next moment the stairway was alive with pounding feet and cries of alarm as each child scrambled downstairs to find his mother.

Olivia was already on her way to the back door when Clay-Boy, followed by the children, ran into the kitchen.

"What in God's name is it?" he cried.

His mother's face was twisted with worry.

"It sounds like your daddy, but I don't know!"

The children stopped their onrush and huddled together at the living room door as Olivia unlocked the back door and apprehensively swung it open. Framed in the doorway was Clay Spencer, half-frozen, an impish grin on his face, his arms overflowing with bundles.

"I've been worried sick about you," said Olivia but her voice broke, and she buried her face in her hands and wept.

"Mama, don't cry," said Clay-Boy. "He's home!"

Struggling with packages, Clay entered. He placed his bundles down on the table, knelt and opened his arms and immediately they were filled with children, brushing the snow from his face, hugging him around the neck, crushing his chest with their frantic embraces.

Now he rose and the children watched with delight as he crossed the floor to Olivia. He kissed her tenderly on the cheek, but then, and this was what the children were waiting for, he picked her up and danced about the kitchen shouting joyously, "God, what a woman I married!" while Olivia shouted indignantly, "Put me down, you old fool!"

Finally he placed her back on the floor. Olivia adjusted her clothing with mock annoyance and demanded, "Where in the world have you been?"

"I missed the last bus out of Charlottesville, so I

hitchhiked to Hickory Creek. From there it was every blessed step of the way on foot."

"Well, you must be nearly frozen. I've been keepen coffee warm." Olivia went to get cup and saucer, and poured the coffee. Clay took his seat at the head of the kitchen table and grinned as he saw the children casting appraising glances at the packages.

"What's in them bundles, Daddy?" asked Luke.

"Beats the tar out of me," replied Clay.

"Where'd they come from?" asked Shirley.

"Well, I'll tell you," said Clay, lowering his voice confidentially. "I was comen up the walk there a minute ago, knowen you kids were asleep, I tried not to make any noise. All of a sudden somethen come flyen across the sky and landed right on top of the house."

"We heard it!" cried Mark and John.

"Well, I looked up and there was a team of some kind of animals about the size of a year-old calf. Somethen kind of pointy on the heads."

"Reindeer," supplied Pattie-Cake.

"I never saw one, but that's what it was all right. Well, it kind of stopped me in my tracks, and I just stood there watchen. First thing I see, this old son-of-a-gun jumped out, all dressed up in black boots and a red suit trimmed with white fur."

"Santa Claus!" whispered John.

"Well, I never laid eyes on the old poot before. Didn't know who he was. I just thought it was somebody tryen to break into the house, so I picked up the biggest rock I could find, and . . ."

Horror stared back at him. "You hit him with a rock!"

"Not exactly, but I scared him so that the sleigh started slippen off the roof and landed right out there in the backyard. The old man in the red suit started cracken the whip and called for them reindeer to take off, but I caught up with him just before that sleigh left the ground."

"You talked to him?" asked Pattie-Cake wonderingly.

"No, but I wrassled him, and just before he got away I grabbed a big armful of stuff from the sleigh and there it is right on the table."

"You see!" said Pattie-Cake victoriously to Becky. "He's real!"

"You're right, honey," nodded Becky with a smile. "You're double-durned right."

"Which one is mine?" asked Pattie-Cake, touching the packages shyly.

"Try that one," said Clay, pointing to a package. "And this one's for you, and this one's for you," he said until all the bundles had been passed out, except one which stood alone.

Cries and shrieks of joy filled the room as Pattie-Cake removed a brand new golden-haired doll which cried and opened and closed its eyes. Becky and Shirley were holding up brand new dresses, and each of the children uncovered treasure after treasure as they went deeper and deeper into their packages: monkeys that magically climbed up strings, teddy bears with soft fur and button noses, jumping jacks which performed virtuoso acrobatics, jack-knives with so many blades that when they opened they resembled a Chinese fan, bouncing balls that jingled, banks in the form of mules which kicked when a penny was inserted, cookie cutters and tea sets, catcher's mitts and footballs, balloons and whistles and spinning tops, and firecrackers and warm socks, and boxes of puzzles and oranges and nuts and candies and still the bottoms of the bags were not yet reached.

"Open yours, son," said Clay to Clay-Boy, who held his package in his arms while he watched his brothers and sisters exclaim with breathless astonishment as they discovered each new treasure.

Self-consciously Clay-Boy tore the wrapper open and he looked at his father with confusion and gratitude and questioning eyes as he found five tablets of good writing paper and a brand new fountain pen.

"I wonder how news got all the way to the North Pole that you wanted to be a writer," said Clay with a grin.

"I guess he's a right smart man," said Clay-Boy, his throat almost too full to speak.

"This one must be for you," said Clay to Olivia, pointing to the one package still remaining on the table.

"What in the world could it be?"

"You been wishen for springtime," said Clay, and placed the package in her hands.

"Oh, Clay," cried Olivia and gazed down at a flower pot containing three hyacinths, one blue, one white, and one rose and all in full bloom.

Pattie-Cake, cradling her doll in her arms, suddenly became aware of something which saddened her, and her lips quivered.

"You didn't get nothen, Daddy," she said. Gently Clay lifted the little girl in his arms and looked around the room at his family.

"Sweetheart," he said, "I've got Christmas every day of my life in you kids and your mama." He turned to Olivia. "Did you ever see such thoroughbreds?"

"I see some sleepy children," said Olivia. "Off to bed now. You can play in the mornen."

"Can't I shoot just one firecracker, Mama?" pleaded Matt.

Olivia considered, but then she smiled and unexpectedly answered "Yes." It'll wake everybody within ten miles, she thought, but she didn't care. Let the world know that Clay Spencer was home.

As the children filed out onto the back porch to
watch Matt light the firecracker, Olivia came and sat
across from Clay. She looked at him, and then at the
hyacinths, and reproach would not come.

"You must have spent every cent of the paycheck,"
she said. She tried to sound cross but somehow she
didn't succeed.

"Just about," he admitted cheerfully.

"What are we goen to live on this comen week?"
she asked.

"Love, woman," he said, and this time he did not
seize her in his arms and waltz madly about the room,
but kissed her gently and took her hand in his.

"BOOM!" went the five-inch firecracker, and
"boom" it resounded across the hills, falling away into
the distance like thunder. Now the children came running into the house, their faces alight with the excitement of it all.

"Bed time," said their father, and with only a few
objections the children marched upstairs and pulled
the covers once more over their heads.

But nobody went to sleep.

They waited until they heard the familiar sounds of
lights being turned off down stairs, the passage of their
mother and father down the hall to their bedroom, and
the click of the light being switched off.

From the girls' room Becky called, "Good night,

Luke," and Luke answered, "Good night, Becky; good night, Pattie-Cake." And Pattie-Cake called, "Good night, Luke; good night, Mama."

And Olivia answered, "Good night, Pattie-Cake; good night, Shirley." Other voices joined in a round song of good nights until all the people in the house had said so many good nights that they could not remember whom they had said good night to and whom they had not. To keep the whole good-night chorus from starting all over again, Clay called "Good night, everybody, and Merry Christmas!" and gave a long sleepy yawn, which was the signal that everyone had been bidden a proper good night. The house fell silent and they slept.

Around the house the world lay bright as day. The moon blazed down its cold light on an earth that was touched with magic. An ancient wind sighed along the ridges of crusted snow. Angels sang, and the stars danced in the sky.

OLIVIA'S APPLESAUCE CAKE

1 cup of butter	3 ½ cups flour (sifted)
1 cup sugar	2 eggs
2 cups applesauce	1 teaspoon cinnamon
2 cups light raisins	2 teaspoons cloves
1 cup chopped walnuts	2 teaspoons nutmeg
1 teaspoon baking soda	Pinch of salt

Sift together: Flour, baking soda, salt, cinnamon, cloves and nutmeg. Take ½ cup of flour mixture and stir into the nuts and raisins. Set both aside. Cream butter until whipped soft. Add sugar a little at a time until mixture is smooth. Beat in eggs vigorously. Alternately stir in flour mixture and applesauce. When all mixed together add nuts and raisins and mix well. Pour batter into a well-greased cake mold. Bake in preheated oven at 350° for one hour. Cool ten minutes, then turn out on cake rack. Frost with Whiskey Frosting when cake is cool.

JANE'S WHISKEY FROSTING

¼ cup butter	2 cups powdered sugar
1 tablespoon cream	2 tablespoons whiskey (bourbon)
	Pinch of salt

Cream butter, add sugar and salt, then cream and whiskey. Whip until smooth. Frost cake. Decorate with a sprig of holly.

About the Author

EARL HAMNER, JR., was born in Schuyler, Virginia, a village in the foothills of the Blue Ridge Mountains. His previous books include *Fifty Roads to Town*, *You Can't Get There From Here*, and *Spencer's Mountain*, which was selected by the Reader's Digest Condensed Book Club, has since been translated into ten languages, and was made into a major motion picture starring Henry Fonda and Maureen O'Hara. Mr. Hamner writes extensively for motion pictures and television. His play *Appalachian Autumn* for *CBS Playhouse* won a Christopher Award, and his script for *Heidi* caused a storm of protest when the little orphan girl from the Swiss Alps cut off the televised New York–Oakland football game with one minute to go.

Mr. Hamner is married and lives on a hillside in Studio City, California, with his wife and two children.